ABE IN ARMS

by *PEGI DEITZ SHEA*

YPF
Shea

Abe in Arms
First Edition

ISBN: 978-1-60486-198-3
LCCN: 2009912426

PM Press
PO Box 23912
Oakland, CA 94623
www.pmpress.org

Reach and Teach
29 Mira Vista Court
Daly City, CA 94014
(888) PEACE-40
www.reachandteach.com

Cover art by John Yates
Layout by Kersplebedeb

Printed in the USA on recycled paper

To Susan Kalkhuis-Beam and Ferdinand Kalkhuis, for their gifts of courage, hope and healing to people traumatized by war.

CHAPTER ONE

What's your name, boy?

He stares into the mirrored sunglasses. Words don't come out.

I'll tell you mine, then you tell me yours.

What's behind those mirrors? All he can see is himself. What's inside that camou-flage uniform?

My name is Grant. See, it's easy. Now tell me yours.

He finds a voice. It comes out: James.

"Earth to Abe!"

"Huh? What?"

"I told you to say my name, Abe," Monica insisted. "I love how you say it, like we're in a café in Paris."

Abe parted her curtain of thin braids and found her ear. "Moan ee cah," he said and felt her shiver in his arms.

Monica yanked the car seat lever, and next thing he knew, he was lying on top of her. Giggling, she rubbed his shaved head as if it were a crystal ball.

"Whoa!" he said, doing a push-up. He rolled back onto the driver's seat and gripped the steering wheel.

"What's the matter?" Monica asked, still lying flat.

Abe glanced over. A mile of creamy nougat skin stretched from her low ride jeans up to her pastel yellow shirt. It was the first thing he'd noticed about her body at the indoor track meet. The girls' uniforms looked more like bikinis. It wasn't fair. How could a guy concentrate on hurdles with all these flashing belly buttons and flexing butts?

Monica sat up straight, the seat clanging upright. She straightened her clothes and asked, "Abe, don't you like me?"

"I do! A lot," he replied immediately.

"Then, how come you don't wanna...hook up?"

Abe shrugged. "I just want to take things slow."

Monica muttered, "If we go any slower, we'll be in reverse."

Abe sighed then put his arm around her. He drew her close and kissed her on the forehead.

"Come on, Abe," she coaxed. "That's the way my little brother Jermaine kisses me. Gimme me some of that fur on your chin."

She threw her arms around his neck, pressed against him and sealed his mouth with her lips. He kissed back, but when her hand wandered south, he blurted, "I can't! I'm sorry. It's not you, Monica, really. It's me, I'm sorry."

Monica slipped away from him, and straightened her clothing. "I should be getting home," she said quietly.

"I thought you wanted to go get coffee or something."

"No, I don't think that's a good idea anymore."

Abe muttered, "I'm sorry."

"Me too."

In silence, they waited for the defroster to clear the windows. Abe then drove out of the park and headed toward the Vernon Heights section of town. Even though it was below freezing, it was still Friday night. Guys crowded the lit-up sports complex, basketballs slapping the tar and clanging on rims. Girls, all puffs of steamy gossip, huddled and bounced, trying to stay warm on the sidelines. Cars throbbed with cranked up bass.

"Abe, wait. Let me off here," Monica said.

When Abe threw the car in park, Monica got halfway out. She took a deep breath and asked, "Abe, are you gay?"

Abe's stomach clenched. "What?"

"'Cause, if you are, it would actually make me feel better. You know, like it's not personal, not about me."

"I'm not gay!"

"Well," Monica hesitated a moment, "I heard some things like you and Niko—"

"Niko's my brother!"

Monica shrugged. "Not by blood. Everybody knows you're from Africa."

"This is unreal! Monica, *you* can't believe—" Abe banged his fist against the steering wheel, then punched the roof of the car.

Monica jumped away, her eyes wide, and ran off.

For a few moments, Abe watched her, now smiling with her friends. Suddenly, they glanced back at him and laughed. God, he hated being laughed at—

Laughter is stabbing them, ripping them apart, a pail over their heads, banging against a wall in a school. Steven cries, James clutches Steven's hand.

What had Dr. Carlson told him to do when the horrors of Liberia came flooding back? Quick! "Leave the scene, do something physical, productive, safe, go play soccer...."

Abe gunned the engine of the silver Camry and peeled off. "Screw Monica!"

He drove to the high school, hoping Niko was up for a game of pool. Good timing. Crowds were bubbling out of the basketball game. The girls' team must have won again. Everybody was jumping, screeching, waving their red and gold varsity jackets like lasso ropes. Vernon High had one of the best girls' basketball teams in Maryland. The crowd always contained at least one recruiter from a top college program like Tennessee, Texas, Duke or Connecticut.

Good—there was Niko. With Maria, damn it. This was beat—Niko hanging around with girls, leaving Abe to fend for himself. Niko was becoming a real player. Look at him, laughing. Why was everybody always laughing?

laughing, having a good time, messing with people before killing—

"Remove yourself from danger," Carlson had told him. "Think positive. You're in a race, you're winning." Abe drove to the south side of the school and got out. He climbed the fence and started running on the track. It was hard as cement in this weather. He didn't care. He needed to pound something. At home, he trudged into the shower, letting the near-scalding water wash down his neck and shoulders. The running had loosened the tension everywhere but there. What was he going to do about these flashbacks? He couldn't tell anybody about them. He *definitely* did not want to go back into group therapy. He couldn't handle hearing about other people's crap. He'd had enough of his own. Even if he did go back to group, what would he say? He didn't even understand what these new images and noises meant.

Anyway, he didn't need help. He didn't need Monica. He didn't need anything to distract him from his senior winter and spring track seasons which would pay his way to college. He had to make his own way forward.

After midnight, Niko strolled into the house. The two teenagers had shared a bedroom for four years now, since Dr. George Elders had brought Abe home from Africa. George had been serving with Doctors Without Borders in a refugee camp in Guinea. Abe had escaped the civil warring that had raged for decades in Liberia. After learning that Abe had no surviving family, George adopted him. He was thirteen.

Now Abe was living large—the so-called American dream—complete with a new adoptive mom, Vanessa. Two incomes, two kids, two cars, huge waterfront property, etc. Their house on an inlet of the Chesapeake Bay had plenty of space for Abe and Niko to have separate bedrooms. After a rocky six months, Niko got used to having a big brother. The boys became inseparable. They knocked down the wall between their rooms and converted the space into "Club Elders." Futon couch-beds, a treadmill, free weights, a ping pong table, a couple of arcade games, a roaring sound system, and high def TV. Plus a small fridge, because club members got thirsty and hungry working out or watching football. And the kitchen was allllll the way downstairs on the other side of the house.

"Abe, you awake?" Niko whispered, close enough for Abe to smell the beer on his breath.

"Yeah," Abe said, leaning up on his elbows, "I bet the girls won tonight."

"Damn straight."

"Gimme some numbers," Abe said.

"Sixty-four to forty-one," Niko said with a laugh.

"Oh, a close one for a change."

"Leisha was a monster, another double double with twenty-eight points and ten rebounds, and she blocked six shots." Niko jumped and pretended to dunk a ball down Abe's throat.

Niko enjoyed embellishing his stories. So Abe played dumb and asked, "So, is that who you took out after the game, Leisha?"

"Hah!" Niko blurted, sitting on his bed and kicking off his shoes. "Can you believe Leisha's going out with some white bread from the prep school now? Well—her loss. I got my shorty point guard, Maria, out on the town tonight."

Abe deadpanned, "Out on the town? Which fine dining establishment, Burger King or KFC?"

"Ah, shut your face." Niko let loose a huge belch and threw a smelly sock at his brother. "So, what kind of big night did you have, bro?"

Abe shook his head and sat up.

"Not so hot?"

Abe sighed hard. "Nah. Listen. I don't want to talk about it. I'm going back to sleep."

"Cool," said Niko, going to brush his teeth. But Abe was still sitting up when Niko got back. "Yo, spill it," Niko said, snapping his jersey at Abe.

After Abe told him about the gay rumor, Niko winced. "The down low? Man, I'm going find the kid who started this rumor and beat the shit out of him."

"What if it's a girl?"

"Well, I'm gonna *prove* her rumor false, with her permission, of course."

Abe said, "Nobody's dissing *you*. It's me. I mean, how can I blame them—eight dates in four years? This fifth date with Monica was a record! I don't think there will be a sixth."

"Yeah, I hear you." Niko plopped on his unmade bed. After a few moments, he asked, "Are you...?"

"What? Gay? No! Nothing against gays, I mean, the guys next door, they're great and all..."

"And Mom's friend, Brenda," Niko added. "And if you were like, gay, that would be cool with me, I mean, you're my bro and all. Hey," Niko laughed, "We're sounding way too politically correct. Let's get back to being male pigs."

Abe couldn't help but smile. Niko always cheered him up. They were complete opposites who fit like a nut and a bolt. Niko—the nut of course—was light skinned because Vanessa had some Latina in her. Abe was black as an eight-ball. Niko was glad to get C's, while Abe was the braino. Niko didn't know the word "quiet." Abe was a monk. Niko—beefy, but agile— played fullback in soccer. Abe, tall and wiry, played midfield. In track and field, Niko threw the shot put, discus and javelin, and Abe ran hurdles and sprints.

"Seriously, dog, give me a day or two to circulate a new rumor." Niko fell to his knees and bowed before his brother. "Tribal Man-child, afraid to wound petite American sistuhs, keeps his African spear in its sheath."

"Hah!" Abe flung a weight ball at Niko's head and fell back howling.

CHAPTER TWO

The next morning, Abe leapt out of bed, and put his uniform on. He punched Niko lightly on the shoulder to wake him. When that didn't work, Abe punched harder.

"Owww, that hurts my head," Niko moaned. "Whassup?"

Ugh. Hangover breath. "Come on, you have to get some food in your stomach before the meet."

Niko rolled and folded the pillow over his head. "Get me some ibuprofen and a Gatorade."

"Yo!" Abe whacked him with a pillow. "Slavery is history. So get your fat ass out of bed and get it yourself."

Abe bounded into the kitchen. The low rising sun lit up the painted yellow cabinets and white walls. After Club Elders, the kitchen was the best room in the house—always full of light and good cooking. Abe smelled vanilla flavored-coffee.

Vanessa swooshed over in her thick plaid bathrobe and grizzly bear slippers. Her long, straightened hair was failing to stay in its bun. She was never awake this early on the weekend. What was the deal?

"A special pre-meet treat for my scholar athletes. Granola with bananas and blueberries," Vanessa said, placing glasses on the table, "and freshly squeezed orange juice."

Niko scuffed in sleepily. "Gee, is that really where orange juice comes from—squozen oranges?"

Vanessa placed her hands on Niko's head and squeezed it. "Let's see what comes out of this coconut."

"Ow!" Niko whined. "Everybody's hurting me this morning."

Abe chuckled. He liked Vanessa a lot. She had the same fun personality his own mother had had before the war in Liberia intensified. How many mothers would challenge the neighborhood kids to a soccer shoot-out, and win! Abe smiled at the memory. Like his mom, Vanessa was always game for anything.

George shuffled in and kissed the boys on top of their heads. Vanessa got a hug from behind. "Mmmmmm," George purred, nuzzling her hair completely out of the bun.

"Coming to our quad-meet, Dad?" Niko asked. "It starts at ten."

"Sorry, guys," George said, pouring a cup of coffee. "I'm on call this weekend, and you know what that's like."

"Yeah," Abe said, disappointed. "See you Monday."

And right on cue, George's beeper went off. Vanessa quickly made breakfast-to-go for him, smearing cream cheese over a bagel, and transferring his coffee into a travel cup.

"Nik, we gotta go, too," said Abe. He threw two sports drinks and a couple of PowerBars into his equipment bag.

"See you over there!" Vanessa called as they rushed out the back door.

At the huge gym, Abe stretched with the other sprinters and with Khalid, his closest hurdling competitor. The girls' team warmed up close by and Abe spied Monica. Should he nod at her or ignore her? He didn't know what to do or say. He'd never had a fight with a girlfriend before. He'd never *had* a girlfriend before.

Abe's hamstrings felt tight as steel cable. Probably from those three miles on the track last night. Stupid! Before doing a hurdle stretch, he massaged the back of his thigh. A murmuring came from behind: "Abraham Elders?" It gave him goose bumps.

"Monica?" he choked out. He hated how her breath could make him feel dizzy.

"Can we talk—alone, over there," she said pointing to the high jump area.

Niko caught Abe's attention and mouthed, "Be cool."

Abe followed her over, willing himself, "stay in control."

They sank deeply into the landing mat under the bar.

She started fast. "Listen, I'm sorry for being so pushy on you last night, and asking, you know, that question. I hope you weren't too pissed at me."

Abe shrugged a shoulder. "Pissed" wasn't all he'd felt. Embarrassed, confused, weak, not that he'd admit all that.

Monica fiddled with the drawstring on her sweatpants. "Late last night, I talked a while with my sister—she's home from college for the weekend—she's a psych major. She said you're probably too sensitive from, you know, the war and all, and losing your whole family."

Abe huffed. That wasn't it. Everybody thought they had the answers. Anyway, he was over that stuff. Meeting George had given him a new life. Getting therapy right after he'd gotten to America had helped him cope.

When Abe didn't reply, Monica continued, "My sister told me, 'If you really like him, you should give him more time.'"

Abe grinned, only on the inside. Thank God for sisters. "So," he said, giving up a mere fraction of control, "are we still going out or what?"

"If you still want to," she said.

"I'll think about it," he droned. Then his voice got deep. "One thing's for sure—"

"What?" Monica asked, with a coy smile.

Abe bounced up off the mat and faced her. "Don't you ever accuse me of being gay and don't be getting everybody laughing at me again."

Monica's mouth dropped in shock. As Abe headed to the track, he heard, "I'm sorry!"

"Moan ee cah," he said silently.

The 55-meter hurdles event always came first. The aluminum hurdles were so big and unwieldy, that the officials needed time to set them up precisely before the meet began. The first indoor meet last month was a fiasco. Abe was leading going over the fourth hurdle, then the fifth one came too soon after. The officials had lined up the hurdles a foot short! All the runners fell over them. The guy in last place ended up winning. He'd seen what happened and just jumped over the mess of hurdles and bodies on the track. Abe's coach argued for a re-race, but the meet went

on. That loss ruined Abe's undefeated season before it
even began.

Abe jogged over the hurdles, getting loose, keeping
his knees high. Coach was talking to that guy from
Temple again. Temple was one of the three schools
Abe visited last summer. The recruiter lifted his chin
and grinned. Abe curtly nodded back. Abe couldn't
keep the NCAA rules straight—"contact period," "quiet
period," "dead period," huh, nice term, "dead period."

Now, as he and his opponents set up in their starting blocks, Abe spied Monica near the finish line.
She'd pulled off her warm-ups and was looking fine in
her red and gold crop top. Wow, he recalled, *she* apol-
ogized to *me!* Hey—snap back, he scolded himself.
He'd have serious competition today, not only from
Khalid. The guy racing in the other center lane had
legs up to his ears. Last time they raced, the officials
had to watch the slow motion video to announce that
Abe did in fact take first place.

The official took his position at the starting line. He
raised his gun straight up and said, "Runners, take
your mark...CLICK."

Abe had bolted, not realizing the gun hadn't
worked. He was already over the second hurdle before
he could slow down. The runners reassembled at the
starting line and got back into their blocks.

"Sorry. Let's try this again," said the official.
"Runners, take your mark... BANG!"

*BANG BANG BANG BANG the rebels pull
everybody into the street, the smallest act
of resistance and BANG, anybody running
away, BANG, grandparents who couldn't
walk fast enough, BANG. A soldier yanks*

*a mother from her home. A girl, clutching a
pink stuffed bunny, follows.*

*Where's your husband? The soldier asks
the woman.*

I don't know.

Who's he fighting for?

*I don't know! You rebels—you're allies one
day and enemies the next day.*

*The soldier slaps her face, spits, Whore!
Well, you're nice and plump. You probably
make a good cook! I'll let you live, let you
live, let you live...*

"Abe, can you hear me? Are you okay? Come on,
Abe, snap out of it."

It was Coach's voice, an urgent and frightened
voice. Abe blinked a few times and found himself lying
on his side, hugging his knees. Someone turned him
on his back. The ceiling lights blinded him. He threw
his arm over his eyes—so many people, everybody
talking. A man's face eclipsed the lights. He wore a
uniform, not a running one, a blue one. And he was
patting Abe's cheek. He held Abe's wrist.

Then he asked, "What's your name?"

Abe knew the answer but he couldn't make his
mouth say it.

Vanessa's voice: "Abraham Elders. I'm his mother,
and this is Abe's brother."

"Abraham," said the EMT. "Look at me. Keep your
eyes open. Listen, you've had some kind of a black
out. We're taking you to the hospital. Your mother's
coming in the ambulance with us."

Niko and the EMT took Abe's arms, and picked him up. Faces were coming clear as they walked him a few steps toward a gurney. He could think. He could talk again. "Monica...." She was crying and biting her nails.

"I don't need," Abe mumbled and tried to shake free. "No hospital. My race, don't wanna miss my race."

Niko and the EMT tightened their grip. "Man," Niko said, "Your race took place ten minutes ago. Khalid blew everybody away."

"What...?"

They were actually strapping Abe onto the stretcher. They tried to put on an oxygen mask, but he kept shaking his head. Then they strapped his head down.

You're not going anywhere, relax, Grant will take care of everything...

Abe gave up. He rested. He was so tired.

Tat-ta-tat, ta-ta-ta-tat

"Bullets!" Abe tried to sit up, but couldn't.

"It's only gravel, Abe," Vanessa said, holding a strap for balance on the bumpy ride. "We're taking the gravel road out from the school. This way is faster to the hospital."

"Whahappened?" Abe slurred.

"We're not sure yet," Vanessa said. "Do you remember anything?"

"I was in the pit with..."

"Honey, you were at the starting line. And then you were out for about ten minutes. You don't remember the false start with the pistol?"

"No," Abe replied, getting scared. "Where's Niko?"

"He'll be here soon. He was in second place with one more throw, so I told him to finish."

Soon, EMTs wheeled Abe into the emergency room. He felt so dumb. He wasn't hurt or unconscious. He was thinking more clearly. He almost laughed—it was so ridiculous.

"George?" Abe said in surprise.

"Your mom called me. Abe, can you tell me what happened?"

"Everybody keeps asking me that. No!" Abe sighed and closed his eyes. He was tired again, so tired.

While Abe was transferred from the gurney to a bed, George launched into action. He ticked off diagnostic tests on his fingers, and initials streamed from his mouth. "CBC, EKG, an EEG, a CAT and MRI on the head for starters." He ordered a nurse to take Abe's blood pressure, and some blood. He walked to the nurse's station and signed the orders for the tests. This was the first time Abe had seen his father function in a real hospital. The makeshift clinic at the refugee camp was prehistoric compared to this high tech, sterile facility.

The refugee camp. "Liberia...," Abe whispered.

"What, honey?" asked Vanessa as she leaned closer. "What do you mean, 'Liberia'? Did something like this happen to you in Liberia?"

"I don't know. My head is killing me."

"I'll get some Tylenol from a nurse. I'll be right back."

Abe awoke to an annoying sound.

"Time for tests! These won't be painful like the SATs, though," chirped the nurse, with a giggle.

Niko appeared behind the nurse. He made a

sweety-pie face and wagged his head. Abe was too tired to laugh at anybody. He obeyed the nurse, lay back and endured the treks wheeling through the white halls.

Three hours later, Abe had been poked, prodded, and squeezed by every person in the hospital. The loud MRI clanks made his ears ring. The tests exhausted him more than hurdling. At least his mind was now clear.

"Everything is negative," George said with a huge sigh of relief. "Normal."

Vanessa clutched Abe's hand. "Thank God," she whispered. "What were they testing for anyway?"

"You don't want to know. The good news, Abe: you didn't suffer a stroke and you don't have a brain tumor. The not so good news is: we don't know what caused the unconsciousness, or seizure."

Great, Abe thought. Maybe I'm just going crazy. "When can I go home?"

"As soon as I go through the discharge papers," George said.

Sometimes it was handy to have a George as a father. A few minutes later, he returned with Abe's marching orders. "Take it easy, lots of fluids, and no driving for a week—"

"No driving?!" Abe exclaimed. An almost eighteen-year-old without a car was useless.

"We can't take any chances that this might happen again when you're behind the wheel," George explained.

Vanessa gently added, "You could kill someone— Niko, yourself."

Abe shivered. He knew what killing looked like.

CHAPTER THREE

Abe spent the rest of the day in bed, but on Sunday, he felt as fit as ever. It was weird to imagine himself losing it in front of so many people. Monica must have seen it happen. What did she think? She'd left three phone messages on Saturday. Now, 8 a.m., it was too early to call her. Besides, her family spent a zillion hours in church on Sundays.

Abe was surprised to see George at the breakfast table. His father stood and hugged him for about thirty seconds. It felt good and safe, as if nothing could hurt Abe when he was in George's arms.

"I thought you were on call all weekend," Abe said, getting a box of Total raisin bran from the cupboard.

"After what happened yesterday, I wanted to be here with my most important patient," George said. "So I switched with someone. I got home late last night, and checked in on you. I'm glad you're still with us, Son."

"Thanks, George," Abe said. "Me too."

"Before and after you eat, I want to take your blood pressure, pulse and heart rate."

"No problem," Abe said, thinking of his father's "First Aid" kit. He should call it a "First, second and third aid kit." George kept a whole bedroom closet full of medical supplies and small equipment. "Be prepared" was his motto.

A mini-exam later, George pronounced, "Normal. Everything's normal, Abe. Wonderful."

While he ate, Abe read the front page of the newspaper. All politics and war. A headline caught Abe's eye—"More Civil Strife in Congo." He squinted to read the caption under a photo of rebels busting open bags of rice: "Rebels steal emergency provisions to trade on black market for weapons."

After breakfast George checked Abe's vitals again. "Hmmm, your heart rate picked up from seventy-six to eighty-nine. That's quite a jump."

Abe pointed to the newspaper. "Maybe because I was reading that."

George scanned the headlines. "That fighting—all the fighting—is so senseless. ...Abe, do you want to talk some more, you know, about what you saw in Liberia?"

"No." He cleared his bowl, wiped the table clean and began emptying the dishwasher.

George laughed lightly as he brought his coffee mug to the counter. "Ever since I met you, you always had to be busy *doing* something, helping somebody." He took the silverware caddy out of Abe's hands and said, "Let's take a walk."

Abe sighed with resignation.

The two put long coats over their sweats and stuck their feet into boots. After leaving a note for the slug-a-beds Vanessa and Niko, George and Abe headed for the water. To the west, small, snow-covered docks reached like welcoming arms into the half-freshwater inlet. Salty ice edged the water and climbed up the posts. Snow sat evenly on the benches, like icing on a store-bought cake. There were no boats, no crab traps, no empty cases of beer. On this mid-January morning, everything was hibernating. Sometimes Abe wished he had a hole to crawl into.

Two hundred yards east, the public park offered better walking. Abe and George headed there, the sun bathing the gray sky with pink and yellow.

"Since the day I first saw you, you were an early riser, too, like me," George began. "I never got to know any of the refugees but you. I mean, the camp in Guinea took in hundreds of displaced persons a day. Doctors only saw the worst cases."

Abe watched some gulls dip and dive. "I know the patients you mean. The ones who got stuff chopped off."

George cleared his throat. "Yes. We couldn't do much beyond making sure the wounds healed properly and didn't get infected. What frustrated me so much was that people were dying from treatable things like measles and diarrhea. And I thought I was going to cure the world."

Abe preferred not to picture the hollow faces and glazed bulging eyes he'd seen everywhere in Liberia— no matter which side the people were on. "I remember the day you first talked to me," Abe said. "You always jogged at dawn."

"And you were always sitting at the camp gates—"

"Waiting for my mother or sister to come, like angels. I was so pathetic."

So many people he knew had died along the way. After the rebels had brutalized Steven and James in the school, they yanked people from their houses. His sister Eleanor, their mom and their neighbors had been rounded up on the street. They couldn't even take any belongings, but Ellie managed to sneak Bunny out. The toy's pink ears peeked out Ellie's skirt pocket. They were forcibly marched to a deserted college that served as a concentration camp. The rebels had separated the prisoners, keeping the males under guard. They kept the females as servants and "wives." The soldiers moved them again to an empty factory. Abe couldn't bear to imagine how his mother and sister had died. All he could remember was gunfire repeating off walls drilling into his ears. Soon after, Abe escaped to Guinea. He no longer had any reason to stay in Liberia.

George broke into his thoughts. "Every morning I asked you for your name, but you didn't tell me. Actually you didn't say anything for months."

Abe picked up a piece of driftwood and winged it out into the water. "I lost my words. Too many horrible things. Words were useless."

George stopped and stared across the inlet. "You showed me that there were other wounds—wounds you can't describe with words, wounds that take a long long time to heal...if they ever do."

Lay off it, already, Abe thought. George was always tying every little problem to the war. They walked on, Abe searching for better memories. "Do you know why I started jogging with you?"

"Because you wanted to be a doctor like me?"

"Ha! No! Because you had the coolest shoes! I thought if I jogged too, then someone would give me shoes like that!"

George reared back and laughed. "And it worked, too, didn't it? Here you are in America with at least three pairs of running shoes—you got cleats, flats for sprinting, you got another pair for distance—"

"And hey, two other pairs for hanging out!" Abe exclaimed.

George threw his arm around his son's shoulder. "And I thought you started jogging with me because I was nice."

"You brought me gum too."

"What a sucker I was," George sighed.

Abe thought back to the camp in Guinea. The tents weren't as good a shelter as the college camp, but the atmosphere was ten times better. He felt protected, at least. He had hope. Things weren't so crazy unpredictable in Guinea.

Abe grinned, remembering his "work" for George. "Seriously," he said, "I really did like the chores you gave me. Running papers back and forth to Red Cross, boiling water, unloading supplies. The most fun part was babysitting the little kids when their moms were getting treated."

"Yes, you were great with kids—you still are."

"If I kept busy, then I wouldn't think about...things so much. That worked too."

"So...," George gently pried, "What's *not* working now?"

In the distance a bell dinged on a buoy. Abe stopped. "Let's turn around, okay?" he asked. "I'm getting cold."

"Sure," George muttered with disappointment.

They did an about-face and headed home. The sun, now above the horizon, threw their shadows in front of them. Water shushed against the thicker ice five feet out. Abe drifted away from George, each step crackling the icy sand.

When Abe spotted their house—a ship on stilts, it looked like—his shoulders relaxed and a sigh es-

caped. He'd rouse Niko and, after church, maybe Niko
would drive them somewhere. God, not driving was
going to be tough. If Monica couldn't get her family's
car, they'd have to double date. Well, at least that
might take away some of her pressure.

His thoughts of Monica were interrupted by George's
voice. "Abe, Vanessa and I decided that you should
talk to Dr. Carlson again. You need a doctor."

"I am talking to a doctor—you. You were there with
me."

"But I'm not a psychiatrist. I'm not qualified—besides, I think a lot more helpful information will come
out with someone else—"

"I've told you everything already," Abe insisted.
Then he jogged up to the edge of their property.

George caught up and placed his hands on Abe's
shoulders. "Shhh. Listen a moment. Look at how
much we've accomplished so far. With Dr. Carlson's
help, you've handled the adoption fantastic. You can
think and talk about your family without breaking
down. You're doing great in school, in track. But
Vanessa and I feel there's more inside that's bothering
you—and we talked about that even before your seizure. Now we *know* there's more inside. Little things
are making more sense."

"What little things?"

"You've got a temper all of a sudden. And we got a
call from not one, but two teachers who complained
that you're zoning out in class. And truthfully, you've
been acting like a mother hen around the house, trying to control things, to make everything perfectly
neat. It's driving us nuts."

"Oh, come on!" Abe said, shucking himself free. He
walked over to the rope swing hanging from the an-

cient pine tree, and started twisting the cord.

George kept a bit of distance. "You liked Dr. Carlson. You can open up to him more. You don't have to worry that you'll upset us—"

"Upset you—with what? What did I do?"

"This is exactly what I'm talking about—you're sounding defensive already."

Abe pushed out a huge sigh and let the cord unwind. The swing seat spun neatly in place, while the rope bowed outward in a blur. "George," Abe said, his voice subdued. "Nobody is ever going to understand me like you do. Not even Niko."

George walked over to face Abe. "Remember, Carlson's a Vietnam War vet. He's seen it all and, believe me, he understands. He even went through post traumatic stress himself. Do you remember what that is?"

It sounded familiar—psycho jargon. Maybe he'd heard it during the first batch of sessions with Dr. Carlson. Between his therapy, Vanessa's social work cases, and George's job, Abe had absorbed enough health knowledge to graduate from med school.

"You mean the flashbacks, right?" Abe said. With Dr.Carlson, they'd gone into the traumatic sights Abe had seen in the war, the "closure" about his mother and sister's deaths, the jolting first weeks living, adopted, in America.

"PTSD results when people are hurting from what happened in the past. They try to keep the past buried. But since they never really deal with the traumatic event, the wounds keep corroding inside them."

"I *am* dealing with it," Abe insisted, "in my own way."

George gripped the rope swing and stopped its spin. "Abe, I need to do something for your own good."

"You're not going to send me back to Liberia, are you?"

"Oh my God!" George bear-hugged Abe. "How could you ever think that?" he said, his voice cracking. "I love you with all my heart and we want you with us forever."

Abe swallowed the lump in his throat, and stepped back. "Then, what are you going to do?" he asked.

George tilted his head and explained, "Okay, this isn't a suggestion anymore; it's an order from me, your father. You *must* get professional help again. If you don't want it to be Carlson, that's fine. We'll find someone else. But the longer you resist, the longer I'll keep you from driving."

Abe looked away and muttered, "That sucks."

That night Monica breathed into the phone. "I'm so glad you're okay. You scared me!"

I scared myself, Abe admitted silently. He doodled interlocking circles on the message pad and asked, "What did I look like? I don't remember anything, and I can't picture myself flat out."

"Abe—do you really want to hear this, because, well—"

"Yes, everybody else saw it, everybody but me."

Monica hesitated then began. "At first, it looked like you slipped from your blocks and fell forward. But then you—well, your body—thrashed and jerked. You were crying."

"Crying?" Abe squeezed his brow and hung his head. "Man, how am I ever going to live this down?"

"Everybody likes you, Abe. Nobody's going to make fun of you."

Yeah, right. Khalid would bust my ass for sure, Abe thought.

"What's next, Abe? Do you have to see more doctors or take any more tests?"

Abe's doodles evolved into a whirlpool of waves. Should he tell Monica? He'd only known her closely for these past two months. Of course, he'd always known *of* her—she was really popular. She did track year round, and she wrote for the school's online newspaper. But could he trust her?

"Hey, Monica? If a student gave you a secret tip for an important newspaper story, would you ever reveal your source?"

"Of course not! If I did, then no one would ever trust me again."

That's what he'd wanted to hear. Still, he didn't need everyone knowing his business. What *was* his business anyway? I hope Carlson doesn't drag me back into the jungles, Abe dreaded. Maybe I could just talk about school and track and maybe Monica.

"Abe, you there?"

Monica! "Yeah, yeah, I'm here. I think."

CHAPTER FOUR

Monica was right—nobody at school actually teased Abe, but plenty of people asked how he felt. Only about thirty students—other than his team—had attended the track meet, but somehow everyone in the school knew what had happened. Teachers, too, and even one of the janitors. Jeez, Abe thought. Like his blackout was more important than the team breaking the school record for points on Saturday.

Thank God for George. He'd prepped Abe with a reply for all the questions. "Just tell them, 'My new allergy medicine caused it,'" George had said that morning. "That's nice and boring." He'd also pulled some strings with Dr. Carlson, and got Abe an immediate appointment. "Professional courtesy," George had called it.

So Wednesday evening, on his way to a basketball game, Niko dropped Abe off at Dr. Carlson's home office—a small, but elegant modern house. It overlooked the bay.

"Waterfront. Must be a doctor thing," Niko said. "I'll pick you up at half time—around eight-thirty."

"Thanks, big guy," Abe said, walking up to the door.

Dr. Carlson, dressed in a full-length chef's apron covered with stains, appeared in the doorway. He stood as tall as Abe—about 6'2"—but was as wide as Niko. His gray-blond hairline had receded majorly since Abe had seen him last. And Carlson had grown a stupid rat's tail with what hair was left.

"Abe, come on in," he said with a southern accent. He pumped Abe's hand and added, "It's good to see you again."

Of course it was good for *him*, Abe thought. He's getting paid!

"You're just in time to give me a hand with these dishes," Dr. Carlson said, leading Abe down a short hallway.

"Uh, okay," Abe said, thinking, I'm the one who should be getting paid!

"My wife teaches water aerobics on Wednesday nights, so I take care of dinner and cleaning up. Do you mind meeting here at my house instead of my office at the hospital?"

"Nah, this is cool," Abe said, accepting a dry dish towel.

Dr. Carlson plunged his hands into the sudsy sink. "So, catch me up on your life, Abe. I can't believe you're a senior already."

Abe shrugged and muttered, "What do you want to know?"

"Courses, sports, college maybe? Girlfriends, huh?"

"Um, all of the above?"

"Excellent!" Dr. Carlson exclaimed. "A very full life. We'll talk about the present in a little while. I reviewed your file to get a grasp of the situation when you first came here. Getting caught in the middle of a civil war is hell, wherever it happens. And losing your family would devastate anyone, no matter which side you're on. Have you used any of the behavior modification techniques we tried out? The coping mechanisms?"

Abe said, "Yeah, I use them sometimes—you know, like removing myself, focusing on positive stuff, talking things over with George."

"Good. What about journaling?"

Abe placed the platter on the clean kitchen table, and grabbed a silver bowl from the drainer. He spotted some congealed cheese on the edge. He chipped it off with his fingernail and polished the bowl. Examining the new shine, Abe, with his shaved head, looked like a lop-sided bowling ball.

"Abe—journaling? Are you writing down your feelings?"

"Nah."

"How come?"

"I'm just not good at writing. When I get bogged down, I feel like doing something physical like running or punching the heavy bag."

"Or going to group therapy? When was the last time you attended?"

Abe knew Dr. Carlson was going to be pissed. But he had no reason to lie. "A year ago. I tapered off. I wasn't getting anything out of it anymore, plus there was too much crying."

"Okaaayyy." Dr. Carlson pulled the plug in the sink and the bubbly water swooshed down. He untied the apron to reveal a simple blue, button-down shirt and khaki pants. Abe's chart had been wedged between the sugar and flour canisters. The doctor pulled it and jotted a few notes.

Staring right into Abe's eyes, Dr.Carlson asked, "How have you been sleeping?"

"Sleep. What's that?" Abe replied. "I wake up every hour it seems. Sometimes I'm covered with sweat."

"Do you remember your dreams?"

Abe nodded. "It's kind of the same dream over and over. There's always shooting, and me running. Sometimes I run towards the shooting, sometimes away from it. I'm never shot in my dreams, but people all around me—Mom, Ellie— are hit. They scream, and that's what usually wakes me up."

Dr. Carlson nodded, scribbling in Abe's chart. "Hey, you said you feel better when you do something physical. Let's go into the basement. I want to show you my new toy."

Abe followed Dr. Carlson downstairs, and said, "Whoa," when he spotted the nine-foot pool table. The doctor motioned to the stand of pool cues and said, "Choose your weapon, and take a couple of practice shots."

Abe found a simple cue. He didn't like the ornamental ones, or those that had fancy grips. He liked to feel the wood without distraction. He lined up and shot a long ball, a two banker, an extreme cut, and a couple of combos.

"George said you were good at pool, but I didn't think *this* good," the doctor said.

"I can make practice shots, but I stiffen up during games sometimes."

Dr. Carlson warmed up then asked, "Straight or 8-ball."

"Straight to 15," said Abe.

Abe won the lag and chose to break. He sank two balls immediately, and put two more in the pockets before a bank shot failed him.

Dr. Carlson pocketed three. As Abe was chalking

his cue, Dr. Carlson asked, "Refresh my memory, Abe. What was it like growing up in Liberia, before the fighting escalated?"

"It was fun," Abe said, leaning against a bar stool. "I liked school. Weekdays, Mom worked in a bank in Paynesville—that's a town south of Monrovia. After school I looked after Eleanor—Ellie. We usually played soccer with the kids in the neighborhood. She was three years younger than me, but nothing got past her in the goal. She was chubby, but she was fast! At first, my best friend Steven didn't want her to play. But she was gutsy, she didn't back down. She showed him—used to stuff his shots all the time." Abe found himself smiling at the memory, then he cut the eleven into a corner pocket.

"What about on the weekends?" Dr. Carlson said. "Did you go anywhere special, or do anything different?"

"Me and Steven used to hang around the docks and watch the fishermen. Sometimes they gave us a few coins for helping them unload their catch. We went fishing all the time up the channel. We always caught dinner. I was proud of that."

"Of course you were. When did your happiness end, and how?"

Abe lifted his head too soon and mis-hit the cue ball. It curled lazily and scratched in the side pocket.

"Sorry for ruining your concentration," Dr. Carlson said. "Let's take a break. Grab a stool. You want a Pepsi?"

"Sure," Abe said and watched his drink being poured.

Abe was still mulling over the question about happiness. He hadn't thought about happiness much. The warring distorted his childhood memories the way oil burned on water.

Dr. Carlson piped up. "I remember happiness in the army—the friends you made for life, the teamwork, weapons practice and training. That was a good 'ole time, until we got dropped into Vietnam and had to start shooting real people. I remember taking over villages in Vietnam—the hatred in those people's eyes— even villagers we were supposed to protect. And the screams and shrill protests. For us to physically pull them out of their homes, then tear their homes up searching for ammo or VC—how demeaning. The personal invasion they must have felt."

Abe listened, watching ice cubes swirl in his glass.

"When the fighting came to your town, what happened?" the doctor asked. "How did you feel?"

"You're right about the hatred, and I remember feeling edgy, like I was going to die very painfully at any moment."

Dr. Carlson leaned on his stick like a pole. "The threat of pain is sometimes worse than the pain itself."

"You got that right." Abe went on, "When the rebels rousted my mother and Ellie from the house, I yelled, 'Mommy! Run!' The man guarding our group spun and pointed his rifle at me. I lifted my chin, thinking maybe this is how I will die."

"Did that soldier hurt you?"

"No."

"Okay...," Dr. Carlson said. "Were your mother and sister hurt right there?

"Not seriously."

"They died elsewhere. Have any more details come out about that?"

Abe stood abruptly. "Like I told you four years ago, it was crazy. I heard them scream and heard them stop screaming after the gunfire."

"All right, Abe," the doctor said, resuming the pool game. "You feel that you're over the grief, and that you were doing well for the past year or so. What's different now? How can I help you?"

"I don't know. It was George and Vanessa's idea to talk with you," said Abe, drilling the four ball into a corner pocket. He then sank five straight. Dr. Carlson dropped in a few. All along, the only sounds were the scratching of chalk, the clacking of balls, and the plunking of them into the netted pockets. No one spoke. Abe didn't know what to say. Did Carlson charge for the silent time too?

"Okay, so why do George and Vanessa think you need my help?"

Abe walked over to a shelf of liquor and spoke while examining the labels. "I'm getting flashbacks again, new ones with different people. Some talking nice to me, some hurting my friends."

"What happens when you get these flashbacks?" Dr. Carlson asked.

"Freaky things, like losing my temper, blacking out, zoning out—going blank. I got taken to the hospital the time I blacked out—they thought I had a seizure or something. "

"Those are serious symptoms, Abe. I'll get copies of the hospital records and go over them before our next meeting. I'm glad you've come back for help. That's a major step in your healing process—a process that sometimes takes a lifetime."

Healing process, huh. Abe couldn't stand the jargon shrinks used. The school psych talked about "self-actualization" and "hierarchy of needs." Teachers were always using words like "ownership" and "self esteem." Why couldn't they just talk plain?

Abe soon made his 15th ball, and the doctor said, "Good timing! We're all done for tonight. Was this okay, meeting here?"

"It's okay," said Abe, helping to cover the table.

"Good, it's much more comfortable here than my office in the hospital downtown. So come on over next Monday night. I want to see you twice a week to start with. And from now on, I want you to record the flashbacks in a journal so I can read about them."

"I'll try. See you next Monday night," Abe confirmed, as they walked upstairs.

Niko had already parked on the street. Abe trotted to the car and opened the door. There Niko was, beer bottle in one hand, making out with some girl.

"Uh oh," she said, a mass of brown curls swishing around. "Hi Abe."

Abe didn't recognize her face. How did Niko get all these babes?

"You don't look shrunken," she said, then threw back her head in laughter.

Shrunk? Shrink? "Niko, you bastard!" Abe yelled, slamming the door. Pounding down the road, he fumed. How dare Niko bring a date to pick me up here? Somebody I don't even know! Now it's going to be all over the school that I'm a nut case.

Niko pulled the car alongside Abe and lowered the window. "Hey Abe, what are you doing? Come on, get in. It's cold as a witch's tit."

Abe could hear the dopey girl still giggling. He gave Niko the finger, so Niko stepped on the gas and screeched away. Abe suddenly had the urge to hit someone. He found a thick branch half-buried in snow. He dragged it free. Then he whacked it against a tree until the limb splintered into flying pieces.

Around midnight, Abe pretended to sleep as Niko came in and got into bed. Abe stayed silent the next morning. As Niko drove them to school, he finally admitted, "Hey, I'm sorry about last night. It was just a joke. I'm a stupid jerk."

Abe couldn't say, "It's okay." Not this time. He felt like he was going to explode. He elbowed the side of the door, and the words came out: "I'm messed up, and you and that girl think it's funny. Why the hell did you bring her along anyway? You know I wanted to keep this psycho stuff private! Who knows who she's going to talk to.... I trusted you, bro."

"I'm sorry," he said, keeping his eyes on the road. "My bad. Sorry."

"Right," said Abc looking out the side window.

Niko pleaded, "Don't be pissed. I'll tell her to keep her trap shut, or I'll never take her out again."

"Great," Abe said, his voice cold as the barrel of a gun.

CHAPTER FIVE

Good thing Abe didn't see Monica until lunch time. He had calmed down by then. After paying for his sandwich, he saw her waving him over. Abe's eyes bugged out when he saw her dark green dress.

"Wow, what's the occasion for the fancy threads?"

"I'm interviewing for a summer internship at the *Daily Journal!*"

"You'll knock them dead," said Abe. "You're an awesome writer."

Monica beamed. "Thanks. I already have a pen name, thanks to you: Monique."

"Monique—that's sounding Frenchy."

"Well, I do have Creole in me."

Monica dabbed at her salad, carefully segregating the purple cabbage slices to the side. Abe grabbed them, opened his sandwich and placed them on top. He hated when people wasted food. They'd never waste anything if they'd ever experienced famine.

"How can you stand those things?" Monica asked. "To me, they look like fresh scars without the skin!"

Abe pretended to gag. "Thanks for smothering my

appetite." Then he took another huge bite right in her face.

As he chewed, he looked around the caf. The Indians and Pakies ate together, even though their countries hated each other. The Jewish kids sat at one end of the caf, and the Muslims stayed at the far end. So much for a melting pot. Abe spotted Khalid— the team's other hurdler and relay anchor. He was only a sophomore, but man, did he push Abe. Khalid was always breathing down his neck. Seeing Khalid messing around with his buds reminded Abe that in ninety minutes, he had his first track practice back since his episode.

Swallowing a tomato slice, Abe asked Monica, "So if you've got an interview this afternoon, that means you'll miss track practice?"

Monica held up her bread stick, until she finished chewing. "Right. I already cleared it with my coach. Why you want to know?"

"I guess I could walk in with Niko. Nobody had better laugh at me."

"Oh, Abe," she said, reaching for his hand across the table, "don't worry about it. Everything will go all right."

"Yeah, I guess. There aren't any starting pistols at practice, so maybe I won't freak out again."

Abe sighed. They had another meet coming up this Saturday. What was he going to do then?

"Hey, why don't you get some ear plugs to muffle the sound?" Monica suggested. "And maybe you can line up in the lane farthest away from the starter."

Abe couldn't believe how well she read his mind. "That's a good idea."

As they continued eating, Abe saw Monica wave

and motion someone over. But nobody came.

"That's strange," she said. "Niko chose to sit with the techies. What's up with that?"

"Maybe he wants a movie done on him. He's so self-centered."

Monica halted her fork in mid-air. "Now where did that come from?"

Abe told Monica about last night.

"That sucks," Monica said. "But you can't stay mad forever. You gotta live with the guy."

"I know," Abe said. But for some reason, he still felt pissed. He usually got over things pretty fast, and was quick to forgive. The last episode, in September, Niko set Abe up on a double date. Without even asking, the girl lit up a joint the size of California. And Abe was driving! He could have lost his license if they'd gotten caught. Niko claimed he didn't know much about those girls, and Abe believed him. After all, Niko wasn't the brightest bulb in the pack. This time, though, Niko's actions were like a betrayal, and ignorance wasn't any excuse. Abe's neck and shoulder muscles cinched at the fresh memory. If he'd been an animal, his hackles would still be raised.

The bell rang and Abe walked Monica to her locker. They had social studies together. Sitting next to Monica for forty-five minutes was worth putting up with their teacher, Miss Blalock. Abe thought that social studies teachers, of all people, should have open minds. But Miss Blalock saw everything as black and white, wrong and right. And America was always right. Abe glanced around the room. The class had kids from all over the world— Latinos who came from Puerto Rico and Mexico. Chinese, or Japanese— whatever—Asians. He couldn't tell if one kid was

Syrian or Saudi. Did they feel the same way—like Miss Blalock? To Abe, everything fell somewhere in between black and white, wrong and right. Nothing, nobody was pure.

"Liberia," Abe suddenly heard. He glanced up from his doodling and saw the class facing him. Miss Blalock was staring at him, but her pointer was stabbing at Liberia on a pull-down map. How the hell did Miss Blalock go from pre-Civil War South to the west coast of Africa?

"Abe? Are you there?"

The class laughed. "Maybe he's seizing up on us again," someone snickered.

"Yeah, Abe, seize the day already."

Abe speared the two guys with his eyes, and clenched his fists. Monica placed her hand over his and whispered, "They're A-holes, Abe. Don't let them bother you."

"That's enough, class," Miss Blalock announced. "There will be no making fun of people with disabilities."

Abe gritted his teeth. Now he's disabled?

As the students quieted, Miss Blalock continued. "I was wondering, Abe, if you could compare our Civil War with Liberia's, since you're a victim of war yourself."

Now he was a victim! Abe couldn't believe this teacher. "I was little," he muttered. "I don't remember anything."

Miss Blalock put her pointer on her desk and walked down the aisle toward Abe. "But surely, you must have learned something. Your parents and their friends would have talked about the fighting."

"My parents are dead."

"Oh, that's right, Abe. I'm sorry," she said with sympathy. But she persisted, "Did your teachers discuss what was going on? Like we do with current events?"

Abe took a deep breath to calm himself. "We didn't have school all the time—"

"All right!" said one of the A-Holes. "I could get used to that."

Abe shook his head in disgust. "Rebels used the schools as bases, sometimes, or prison camps. Other times we'd get word to stay in school because it was the *only* safe place. Once, I spent three days straight in school while rebels burned our homes and killed unarmed people in their own houses."

Nobody had anything funny to say at that.

"What about what caused the war? I remember reading that jungle tribes were attacking the educated people, the government and the business people," she said. "That's different than what happened in the U.S."

Abe tried to stay in control. He belonged to one of "those jungle tribes," the Gio. And he had never lived in a jungle—he lived in a real house, like most people did. Not all people were savages; and not all savages were that way all the time. War changed people.

"The Liberian civil *wars*," he said, emphasizing the plural, "were more like the battles between Native Americans and European colonists. Not North versus South."

Miss Blalock folded her arms and said, "But Liberia wasn't exactly colonized. America returned many slaves to Africa, and they founded Liberia in 1820. They even named their capital, Monrovia, after our president, James Monroe."

How stupid could she be? Abe stood, now looking down at her. "Listen, the tribes didn't need any 'founding.' They were there the whole time. And the ex-slaves treated the tribes like slaves." Abe's voice rose. "Just like with the Indians, the 'Americans' stole our land, didn't let us use our languages, didn't let us get education. Before we were 'Liberians,'" he yelled, pounding his fist into his hand, "we were Kru, we were Khran, we were Mano, we were Grebo, we were—I am Gio."

The whole class had held its breath. Blalock stumbled backward, her fingers to her lips. Abe gazed around the room, daring someone to breathe, to speak. Monica wouldn't meet his eyes.

Finally the teacher's voice crackled, "Thank you, Abe, for the, um, history lesson."

Abe felt like he was drowning, like he was going to be sucked under by another dark flashback. He hadn't had one in five days. And he wouldn't have it happen again, especially not here. He had to get out of there, "remove" himself from the danger.

He clutched his books like life preservers to his chest. He stormed out into the hall, and kicked dents into a bank of lockers. A couple making out fled around the corner. Abe banged open the boys' room door, dropped his books and blasted the cold water. Over and over he doused his face. He didn't know if he was going to laugh or cry. He leaned his forearms on the sink, and it groaned away from the wall. He let up, got some paper towels and dried his face.

"I am Gio," he breathed at the mirror. "I am Gio."

Suddenly the school security guard came in, the vice principal behind him.

"Mr. Elders, harassing a teacher and storming out of class isn't like you," said Mr. Sloan.

"I know, I'm sorry I lost my temper, but she...was lying about Africans, she's so... ignorant!"

The vice principal gave a chuckle. "To tell you the truth, she doesn't get the best evaluations, but she has tenure. Let's head over to Guidance and see if we can transfer you. You realize that I'll have to report this and call your home. But since it's your first offense, I don't think you need detention to deter you from further episodes, do you?"

"No sir," Abe mumbled.

A half hour later, Abe waited outside Blalock's front door for Monica. He needed her rational mind. But when the bell rang, Abe watched his girlfriend dart out the back classroom door, and pace directly to the stairwell. She hadn't even looked for him. Probably petrified of him. He knew from her schedule that she was heading downstairs. He was stuck on this floor for his last class. He sank down and flipped to the back of his current events notebook. Under the word: JOURNAL, he wrote the date. He glanced around the hall hoping that someone, anyone, could tell him what to write. Across from him, Abe caught his reflection in the glass door to the courtyard. He looked half dead.

Words seeped onto his page: What is happening to me?

CHAPTER SIX

While the track team was warming up, Niko crept toward Abe like a dog desperate for a pat. And like a dog with nothing better to do, Niko yawned and stretched beside Abe.

"How's it going?" Niko asked, a bit too jovial.

Trying his best to lighten up, Abe gave his brother a little punch in his muscled arm. Niko laughed, a sigh escaping.

"Yo," Abe said, "you didn't tell me you broke the indoor shot put record last Saturday."

Niko bent over and touched his shins—his fingers miles away from his toes. "We weren't exactly focused on our events, remember?"

Abe admitted, "I didn't even notice that you'd left the hospital."

"What was I going to do all afternoon during your tests? Hit on some candy stripers?"

"Exactly," Abe said, grateful for Niko's humor. "Anyway, congratulations. And keep breaking that record. We've got five months of track and field left."

Niko smiled broadly. After stretches, he punched Abe back, then jogged over to the pit.

Coach gathered the sprinters and hurdlers. "Kevin is out indefinitely with a groin pull. That means I need another body for the 800-meter relay. Abe, are you feeling okay? Would you give it a try? You're our next fastest."

"Sure!" Abe immediately replied, excited to do more events. At meets, he'd always get bored after the hurdles went off. He'd catch some field events, but those athletes moved in slow motion, compared to the runners. The relay would keep him fired up. He'd need practice passing the baton, though.

"Great," Coach said. "Abe, go hit the hurdles, and come back to me at three forty-five for relay practice."

Instinctively, Abe searched for Monica around the track. She was a sprinter and relay racer too. Then he remembered she had to leave early for her interview. Now, who was he going to run for? Niko? Coach? For myself, Abe decided. "For I am Gio," he said as if he were an X-man.

He began with a lead leg drill. He ran down the left side of the hurdles, lifting his right knee to clear the hurdle, and snapping it down afterwards. No flying. No time-consuming air. Then, down the right side of the hurdles, he did his trail leg drill—charging with power into his next stride.

As he set his blocks for starts practice, Abe felt keenly aware of every noise in the building—the blaring of Coach's whistle, the thundering of the runners racing around the banked curves, the squawking of the girls' team coach, and the panting of sprinters just past the finish line. It suddenly occurred to him that all these people were running for *fun*—in circles no less— throwing stuff, jumping higher and farther than somebody else. There wasn't any of that

in Liberia. People ran for their lives, they threw gre-
nades, fire bombs, rocks if they had nothing else.
They jumped over dead bodies, not hurdles.

Abe shook his head free of memories. He wasn't
going back, not here and now in another school situation. If it would stop the flashbacks, maybe he'd let
Dr. Carlson take him back into Liberia time. Maybe.

After his practice, Abe joined the relay team. The
baton pass had always seemed easy enough. You ran
full speed and caught up to your teammate who'd just
taken off. Right hand to the next runner's left. Piece a
cake, right? Wrong. The first few times Abe handed off
to the anchor Khalid, Abe dropped the baton.

"Jeez, Abe!" Khalid said in disgust.

"Sorry, man, sorry," Abe said, fumbling to pick the
baton up again.

"Khalid, don't take off so fast," Coach called.

Khalid shook his head. "Sheeet, if I went any slower, we'd come in last."

"Hey, lay off, Khal," Abe said.

Abe finally got the baton passing down, but it was
messy. Once Abe put the wrong hand back to receive,
and he ended up running outside his lane. He would
have disqualified the whole team. Same with the time
he ran too far before receiving the baton.

"Don't worry," Coach said, calling Abe over. "We've
got a lot of time to practice before Saturday. Listen,
another reason I want you to run the relay Saturday
is because college recruiters will be at this meet. One
from Rutgers even."

"That's good, right?" Abe asked, unfamiliar with the
program at Rutgers.

Coach nodded in exaggeration. "Division One—their
hurdlers are NCAA top ten indoor and out. Plus, it's

smart to show him that you can contribute more to
the team in other ways, like relays."

"Wow," Abe muttered. New Jersey wasn't so far
away—just a couple of hours from Maryland. Abe had
partial scholarship offers from several small colleges,
but not one of this stature. Saturday. That gave him
plenty of time to sort things out. He'd have his act together by then.

"Let's get some timed relays in," Coach told the four
runners. He blew his whistle and hollered, "Clear the
inside lane!"

Disgruntled, the middle- and long-distance runners
moved to the outer lanes, making their laps longer.
There was always some tension between the distance
runners and the sprinters. Any race longer than 200
meters bored Abe. Sprinting was more glamorous,
more exciting. Distance runners looked like skinny
robots, while the powerful sprinters had muscles in
their ear lobes.

But when it came to the relays, the whole team so-
lidified. The relays, held at the end of the meet, often
determined which team won.

Abe had watched a hundred relays, but was fuzzy
on the precise rules. "Coach, what lane should I
take?" Abe asked.

"During a race, it depends on if we're in the lead. If
we're in second place, you get or pass the baton in the
second lane. Same thing for third place. But as soon
as you get the baton, you can run in the inside lane.
We'll just use the inside right now for practice."

The first runner ran the first leg of the relay only
half a second off their fastest pace, Coach said, timing
the splits. As the second runner was halfway around
the track, Coach told Abe, "Get ready—a standing

start—I'll say 'go' when I want you to begin running. ...Ready...go!"

Abe dug his toes into the track and coached himself: "Step one,two,three, left hand back, get the baton, bring it up, switch to right hand. Dash!"

It went smooth! It worked! Abe churned up the track. He used the curves like catapults into the straight-aways. This was fun. He never got to run curves in indoor hurdling. And the outdoor track wasn't banked like this. Before he knew it, Abe had to hand off. He ran full speed to catch up with Khalid, then slapped Khalid's hand with the baton.

"Yow," Khalid yelled.

"Grow up, ya baby!" Coach called. Under his breath, he told Abe, "Not so hard next time. You don't want to distract the runner from his job."

"Gotcha," said Abe.

When Khalid crossed the finish line, Coach growled, "Two whole seconds off pace. Let's improve upon this, Ladies. Again, two more, timed!" Coach ordered, handing the stopwatch to an assistant. Then he headed over to the shot put pit.

Without Coach there giving Abe tips and cutting him some slack, Abe felt uneasy. The first time alone, Abe fumbled with the baton like a hot potato. They ran 2.5 seconds behind pace. The second handoff went better, but as he approached Khalid, Abe was running too fast. The front of his spikes caught Khalid in the Achilles tendon.

"Oww!" Khalid yelled, hopping on one foot over to the bleachers. "Don't run up my fucking back!"

Abe yelled, "And you get off my case. I'm just learning."

Khalid strutted over and bumped chests with Abe.

"Learning to be what? A big excuse maker, kissin'
up to Coach's ass?" Khalid jabbed his index finger
into Abe's chest. "What excuse you gonna give when I
whup your ass in hurdles Saturday, huh?"

I don't feel good. Better tell somebody. Better remove myself.

The flecks of gold twinkling in Khalid's brown eyes
infuriated Abe. He swung and caught Khalid hard
in the right brow. Khalid staggered backward and
fell into the thick high jump mat right as a jumper,
Kaitlin, was elevating to the bar. Seeing Khalid, she
knocked the bar down, which landed between her and
Khalid. Both cried out in pain.

Coach came running. "What the hell is going on?"

Khalid gasped, "Nothing, Coach."

"Don't say 'nothing,' Khalid," said Kaitlin. "Look at
this red gash along the back of my thighs!"

Khalid, staring at Abe, said in a monotone, "A couple of Khalid kisses will take care of that, sugar." The
bit of humor saved him face in front of the girls' team.

"Practice is over. You two," Coach said, pointing at
Abe and Khalid, "in my office in twenty minutes."

When Abe got out of the shower, the boys' locker
room was buzzing. Abe couldn't be seen in his cubicle, but he heard everything. He couldn't help feeling
some pride with his tough new reputation.

"What a shot!"

"Abe never loses his temper. Did you see what
happened?"

"No, but I heard about it. So Abe knocked Khalid's
teeth out?"

"And Khalid's eyes teared up bigtime."

"Man, I wish I was pinned under Kaitlin."

Abe laughed at that one—Kaitlin *was* hot.

Before he reported to Coach's office, Abe scribbled in his journal:

"Smashing Khalid felt great. He deserved it. He had it coming."

Coach already had Khalid sitting in the office by the time Abe arrived. There wasn't another seat, so he stood in the doorway. Coach, on the phone, acknowledged Abe's presence and held one finger up. Holding an ice pack to his right eye, Khalid pouted straight ahead at the wall.

Abe had been in Coach's office for short pep talks before, but he'd never checked out the fine print. A bunch of certificates hung on the tan cinder block wall—a diploma from Springfield College, a Massachusetts school noted for its phys ed program. A Masters in Health Education from MSU. Framed photos of Coach throwing the javelin, the shot put and discus for Rutgers. God, he looked funny—bushy hair, short shorts up his butt, ugly scarlet sweat suits. Then there was the trophy filled shelf. State High School Champion in javelin in 1978, Atlantic College Conference champ in '80, '81, and '82. All that was missing was an Olympic medal.

Coach hung up the phone, and looked back and forth between Khalid and Abe. His eyes finally settled on Abe.

"I'm disappointed in you," Coach began. "You're a senior, you're co-captain, and you do something childish like punching a team mate. Worse—a relay team mate when we're already down one runner! What do you have to say?"

"Sorry, Coach, it was stupid," he admitted.

"Khalid, my assistant coach said you were coming down pretty hard on Abe when he made mistakes.

Everybody makes mistakes. Nobody's perfect. *You're not perfect.*"

Khalid sighed heavily, cocking his head to the left.

"Now, I'm willing to forget what happened, to not file an incident report to the vice principal *if* you fellas shake hands and apologize to each other. And *if* you guys show me how to work as a team from now on. We fight together. We don't fight ourselves."

Next time I see such a crime—!

Abe blinked the words away.

"Now, shake hands!" Coach ordered.

Abe stuck his hand right in front of Khalid's nose. "Sorry, man," he said.

Khalid slapped Abe's hand and muttered, "Yeah, sorry."

"All right, you sorry goats, get outta here."

Niko was waiting in the locker cubicle when Abe returned. "Hey, what happened? Tell me everything."

Abe sat on the bench and leaned his elbows on his knees. "I don't know, Nik. It's like one second I was real calm and sorry about messing up the relay and all, and the next second I wanted to tear Khalid's head off. What's scary is that I didn't want to stop. If it wasn't for Kaitlin falling on top of him, I *would* have torn his head off."

Niko rubbed his chin and sat next to Abe. "Man, I hope I never do anything to get you *that* mad."

"Huh!" *If only he saw me last night.*

CHAPTER SEVEN

Vanessa and George had some fancy banquet they had to attend, so Abe and Niko stopped at Pizza Joint before going home. Niko devoured a medium sausage and onion pizza all by himself, while Abe got a spinach calzone.

Abe's phone rang. Before he could even put it to his ear, he heard, "I got it! I got it!"

"Excellent! That's really great news!" Abe covered the phone and told Niko, "Monica's got a newspaper internship for the summer."

"Summer?" Niko said. "Summer is for VA Beach."

"Let's celebrate!" Monica said. "I'm only a mile away from your house. Can we meet there?"

"Sure," Abe said. "We're at Pizza Joint. Want me to bring you some dinner?"

"That's so sweet! Can you get me a personal pie— vegetarian, okay?"

Monica was waiting on the porch when Niko and Abe arrived. Abe gave her a big hug and said, "Didn't I say you were going to knock 'em dead?"

"The Journal editor really liked the investigative

piece I did on our school being vandalized last year."

"Hey, I remember that issue of the 'Sailcloth.' You wrote that?" Abe asked.

"Uh huh," she said, taking off her down jacket. "During the interview, the editor had me write a test news story. He gave me a list of facts that were chronologically jumbled up. He said I was the only one who got the order right. I even invented quotations."

"Maybe I can use that technique on my next research paper," said Niko, heading upstairs.

Abe gave Monica her pizza and they sat in the breakfast nook. "How did you do on the civics part of the test?" Abe asked. "You were nervous about that."

Monica, her mouth full, mumbled, "The only one I couldn't come up with was P—"

Abe felt something wet hit his cheek. "Yo, keep your food to yourself!"

"Oh my God! I'm so sorry! What a pig I am!"

"Don't worry!" Abe laughed, reaching up.

"No, I got it," Monica insisted, wiping Abe's face with her napkin. "It was some onion—good thing you like them!"

"Good thing the editor didn't test you on your manners!" Abe said.

After she finished, Abe got the nerve to ask, "Want to hang out a while?"

"Sure, I finished my homework in study hall."

"Great," Abe answered, clearing the table. "I have a paper due, but not until Monday."

After Monica called her folks, Abe led her upstairs to the rec room. Niko was already playing on an arcade game.

"Wow!" she sighed, "a real boy's club." She selected some tunes, and walked over to a game unit. "What the heck is this?" She asked. "It looks like a computer from that old show, 'Lost in Space.'"

Niko called over, "It's called Honky Dong!"

Monica's mouth dropped open. "What?"

Abe laughed. "The game is called 'Donkey Kong'" and that's George's old Atari. There's also a game called "Pong," as in ping pong, and all it is a ball bouncing side to side.

"It's a freaking dinosaur egg!" Niko commented.

"Then I'll leave it alone." Monica sashayed over to a different game. "Hey, I've always wanted to try those water gun races at carnivals, but my dad never lets me. He said all those games are rigged and you just waste your money all for a neon, stuffed monkey."

"Well, here you don't have to put in any money, and the gun is a laser. Try it!" Abe said. "Aim at those animals—it's like a safari."

Monica took the attached gun and placed her finger on the trigger. She started waving the gun all over the place, and she only bagged one lion. "I stink at this," she giggled.

"Let me help you with your timing," Abe said. He stood behind her and put his arms around her to guide the laser gun.

"Oooo," Monica whispered, leaning back into him. "I like this kind of help."

Abe shivered and kissed her neck. She started to turn toward him, but he kept her facing the game. He lowered his voice and intoned, "Now, let's concentrate on the mission. Because if you don't get the lion, the lion will, the lion will—"

> *get you, James," the soldier Grant says, standing behind, arms on arms, hands on*

hands. Another soldier is showing Steven how to shoot too. Grant's voice is calm and tickley, "Hold the gun steady now, stay hidden if you can, if not stay low... now the automatic, you can shoot it two ways, if the enemy is moving, aim a bit ahead, then spray left to right, they run right into the bullets, the idiots, if they aren't moving, you become the hunter in the bush, picking off kills as easy as nits, now try shooting that tree, slowly squeeze the trigger and hold, puhpuhpuhpuhpuhpuhpuh. Of course it hurts your shoulder, James. Pain is how you know you're still alive, here, take this, it's something special for the pain, powder candy, go ahead, sniff it up and Steven gets some too, and soon the world slows down and everything brightens....

"Abe? Hellooo? Any signs of life?" Monica asked, gently slapping Abe's face.

Abe snatched her wrist before she could do it again.

"OWW! Abe, not so tight! That hurts," Monica said, wrangling free.

"Yo, Brother!" Niko said, stepping between them. "What's going on?"

Abe blinked a few times and started pounding his own head with his fists. Niko gave him a bear hug, pinning Abe's arms to his sides. He easily picked Abe up and sat him, sagged like a rag doll, on the couch.

Monica had backed up against the far wall. "Is he okay, Niko?"

Abe nodded.

"Does anything hurt?" Niko asked.

He shook his head.

"You really zoned out, dog."

Abe felt like he was going to cry. "Water?" he asked, his breath catching.

While Monica hit the fridge, Abe and Niko stared fearfully into each other's eyes. Niko put his hands on Abe's shuddering shoulders. "It's okay, it's okay. Your brother's right here, and so is your lady."

Monica gave Abe a water bottle, then stepped backward quickly. Abe sucked half of the bottle down. "Want to talk about it, Abe?" Monica asked from a safe distance. "Maybe we can help. Was it like that time—the seizure?"

Abe whispered, "Just a memory—something I'd forgotten about."

"Was it your friends Steven and James again?" Niko asked.

Monica gave Niko a bewildered look. "Friends?"

Niko explained how Abe's friends were abused and taken prisoner. "Abe, I think you'll feel better if you talk."

"Okay, I'll try," he whispered, wiping sweat from his brow. "But nobody's telling anybody else." He shot a warning at Niko and added, "Especially George and Vanessa."

Niko and Monica said, "Promise."

Abe took another swig and began. "Steven and me, and a bunch of us—families, kids—we were being held prisoner at this abandoned college. It was so boring, man, all the books had been burned and the equipment broken. There was nothing to do all day."

Abe drained the water. "Steven and I started talking to this one officer, Grant was his name. He was real easy going—not threatening to slit your throat like some of the wild rebels would actually do for fun. We were told they ate prisoners too."

Monica and Niko grimaced at each other.

"Sick, isn't it?" Abe said. "James persuaded Grant to let us kids outside to run around a bit, play chase or something. That we wouldn't be such pains in the ass if we could let our energy out. So he said 'okay' for the boys, but the soldiers wouldn't let the females out. They were kept on the cafeteria floor, doing laundry, cooking and cleaning. The soldiers made some of them their 'wives.' We were on the third floor; the guards had the second floor."

"How many prisoners were there in that one building?" Monica asked, her voice shaky.

"About 300. There were some other buildings, but I didn't know what they were used for."

"God," Niko said. "What did you have to eat?"

"You *would* think of that," Abe said with a tiny smile. "Mostly rice or bread, and water. But here, I think, is what's twisted. James and Steven and sometimes me got extra...stuff, because of Grant. We would ask us to do chores like cleaning guns, sewing gashes in their clothes. And the guards started treating us better. They even taught us how to shoot the AK47s."

"Shoot?" Monica gasped, her hand to her chest.

Niko looked excited, but sobered up quick when Abe glared at him.

They heard a car pull into the driveway and Niko jumped to check out the window. "Vanessa and George are home early, Abe."

As he got up, Monica asked, "Are you done... talking?"

Abe shrugged and stammered. "I think the gun just now set me off. Anyway, it was just so...wrong of us to get friendly with the rebels. I felt guilty because they were...killing innocent people, and here we were accepting candy from them."

Niko slung his arm around Abe. "You were just a kid, Abe. You didn't know better. Now that shot at Khalid today, that was real rebel stuff."

"I heard about that. *You* beat him up?!" Monica wondered as they walked downstairs.

"It wasn't like that—it was different!" Abe protested.

In the front hallway, Niko started lightening up the situation. "Whoa, Mom!" He said, spinning her in a pirouette. "Dad, you take her out looking this good— that's dangerous."

George laughed and threw their coats over an armchair. "Well, who do we have here?" he asked, extending his hand to Monica.

"This is my friend, Monica LaForge."

Niko cleared his throat for attention, and sang, "Abe's *girl*friend."

Abe quickly piped in, "Monica's going to be a hot shot journalist, that is, after she breaks the Olympic record for the hundred."

"Aw, cut it out," Monica said.

"It's nice to meet you, Monica," Vanessa said. "I think I've met your mother. Is she with the public defender's office?"

Monica nodded. "Yes, ma'm, she does a lot of juvey cases. Abe said you're a social worker? You probably work with some of the same kids."

Vanessa sighed, "Unfortunately, yes."

"Listen, I was just leaving," Monica said. "It was nice to meet you."

"I'll walk you out," Abe said, grabbing her coat.

As they reached her Toyota, Abe leaned against the

door. "I'm sorry about what happened tonight, you know, upstairs. I didn't mean to hurt you. Plus, you shouldn't have to hear about that nasty stuff about Liberia."

Monica quickly opened the door and got in. Her brow creasing, she said, "I should be glad you're telling me these things, Abe, if it helps you feel better."

"Yeah, but I got a doctor to lay it on now, so you—"

"And you'll tell him everything that happened today, right?"

"Yeah, sure, whatever." Abe leaned in for a kiss and met Monica's cheek.

She drove off without saying goodbye, see ya tomorrow. Not a word.

Back inside the house, Niko was play boxing with George, so Abe slipped upstairs. He opened his journal and wrote:

"I hurt Monica shooting. I didn't mean to. She was, like, slapping me and a voice said, 'nobody gets away with that anymore.'"

CHAPTER EIGHT

Track practice Friday went more smoothly. Abe and Khalid ignored each other. Coach had made it easier by switching Abe to second leg in the relay order so he wouldn't have to hand off to Khalid. All this speed practice made Abe feel stronger, faster in the hurdles. He couldn't wait until Saturday when he'd go head to head with Khalid. He wanted to destroy him more than anybody on the other team, Central High.

After practice Friday, Niko had plans, and took the car. Abe found Monica chatting with friends outside the girls' locker room. Seeing Abe, they walked away.

"Can I bum a ride home?" he asked Monica.

"Um, sure, I guess," she said, heading to her car. "Only I have to stop home and check on dinner, so you might want to ask someone else...."

"I'm in no hurry," Abe said, nuzzling her shoulder. She didn't nuzzle back.

Once on the road, Abe asked, "Where were you at lunch today?"

"Oh! I ate in Mrs. Steer's room. We were laying out the next issue of *Sailcloth*."

"And now after my transfer outta Blalock's class, I didn't get to see you until practice. I'm missing you, Moan ee cah,"

Monica gave a nervous laugh. "Me, too."

"How was the old bag, Blalock?"

Though stopped at a red light, Monica answered without looking at Abe. "Oh, you know, same old same old. Remember, she's from Connecticut? She was trying to state that the North never really had slavery. But I raised my hand and said that even the author Mercy Otis Warren in Massachusetts had slaves."

Abe shook his head. "Huh! What did she say then?"

Monica picked up energy and faced Abe. "She backtracked, of course." Monica raised her voice to mimic Ms. Blalock: "'Well, slaves in the North were few and far between. It was definitely the North that pushed for abolition.' Then she went on about Noah Webster—the dictionary guy—how he wrote against slavery even before 1800. I'm going to have to check that out."

A horn honked, startling Monica at the wheel. She grinned into the rear view mirror and said between her teeth, "Keep your pants on, Mr. Wannabe Jeff Gordon."

In a few minutes, they drove into Monica's driveway. "I'll only be a minute—you can stay here."

"And miss meeting the little man Jermaine? Not a chance."

"I don't even know if Jermaine's here."

"Hmmmmm," they said together as they came through the kitchen door. Monica found a note on the table.

"Monny, my turn to drive the car pool for Jermaine's gymnastic lesson. I'll be home around six. DO NOT TOUCH BREAD IN THE MACHINE!"

Monica picked up the lid on the crock pot. "Ma didn't say 'do not touch the soup.'"

"So that's what's cooking?" Abe asked, placing his coat around a chair.

Monica stirred the creamy orange liquid, and they both inhaled the tangy aroma. She took a taste. "Hmm, curried butternut soup—one of my favorites. Want to try?"

Monica started to fetch a new spoon, but Abe put his hand over hers, and dipped the spoon back into the soup. "Why don't you feed me?" he asked. "It will taste better that way."

"Well...," she said and bit her bottom lip, "Okay."

Abe closed his eyes as Monica put the soup in his mouth. His eyes swooned in circles under their lids. A smile opened his face wide.

Now a bit feisty, Monica said, "My turn."

Her voice turned melodic as she demanded, "Another one, and kiss me right after you take the spoon out of my mouth."

What did she have in mind? Abe wondered. He scooped some soup and blew cool air across the surface. "Open wide," he instructed. She did as told and in went the spoon, clicking slightly against her bottom teeth. Abe withdrew the spoon, and then kissed her. Monica's tongue came into his mouth. She shared the soup with him and soon the tawny broth was running down both of their chins. Kissing and giggling, they stumbled into the living room. Monica lightly pushed Abe onto the couch and lay on top of him. Abe let her.

"I just checked Jermaine's schedule. We have a half hour before they come home," Monica whispered.

"Hmmmm," Abe mumbled.

He slid his hands around her waist and under her

shirt. He half-expected something weird to happen. But no memories came crashing down to ruin everything. No flashbacks so far. His hands glided over her smooth skin, stretched taut over her powerful muscles. How could she be soft yet so firm at the same time?

Monica rubbed his bald head and the tops of his shoulders. Then she sat up and unbuttoned his shirt. "Ooo, a smooth chest to match your head," she cooed, as her fingers drummed slightly.

Abe's hands ventured to her breasts. The image of billiard balls popped into his mind and he almost guffawed. He closed his eyes, banishing the thought, and concentrated on Monica.

"Mmmm, Abe, say my name. Make it rumble."

"Moan ee cah," he moaned.

"Again," she whispered, sliding off to the side.

Abe felt jittery and weak. All of a sudden he couldn't speak.

Monica's hand moved down over his tight abs. "Relax," she insisted. "Breathe deep."

Abe took a huge breath, and felt her fiddling with his fly. He froze. "Don't."

"Shhh, don't make a sound. It's going to be good. You'll like it."

Those words, he had heard them before. He sat up straight. "Not today, okay? Not yet."

Monica sighed loudly and sat up. "You're just like that stupid Pong game!"

Abe straightened his clothes and asked, "What do you mean?"

"In your rec room the other day, you practically tore my arm off. But today, you were so gentle and, you know, all lovey. You're going back and forth like the

Pong ball and it's driving me nuts!"

"I'm sorry, I—"

A car door slammed in the garage.

"Oh my God!" Monica said jumping off the couch and buttoning her shirt. "You actually saved us, Abe."

Abe had just finished tucking in his shirt when a little boy tore into the room. "Monny, watch what I learned today!" And he cartwheeled twice across the floor.

Monica and Abe clapped. "Way to go, little man," Abe said.

"Hey, who are you?" Jermaine asked, walking right up to Abe. He looked straight up as if he were standing next to a skyscraper. "You're a lot taller than Monny's last boyfriend!"

"And a lot stronger too," Abe laughed. He picked him up over his head and twirled like a pro wrestler.

Jermaine squealed with glee. When Abe let him down, Jermaine ran to the kitchen, singing, "Monny's got a new boyfriend, Monny's got a new boyfriend."

Monica's mom came in and held her hand out to shake. "Hello new boyfriend," she said. "You must be Abe."

"Nice to meet you, Mrs. LaForge."

Then she kissed her daughter hello and said, "Remember our rule about no guests in the house when I'm not home?"

"Mom, how was I supposed to know you had car pool duty?"

"You got me there," she said, tilting her head. "Abe, I hope Monica invited you for supper."

"Uh, no—"

"Then you'll stay, that is unless you have somewhere you gotta be."

Abe glanced at Monica who gave him a short nod. "Uh, thanks, I'd love to stay. Let me call home first."

At the table, Jermaine took the seat beside Abe. He copied everything Abe did and peppered him with questions. Abe hadn't seen this kind of energy since Ellie. The sudden thought of her made his face go slack. He totally missed one of Jermaine's questions.

"Jermaine, that's enough," Monica said. "Let the poor boy eat his meal!"

When Jermaine pouted, Abe said, "Let's see who finishes eating first." And the boys were off.

Saturday's away meet at Central was just a dual match—boys and girls. For a change, George could make it. He and Vanessa sat in the bleachers on special portable seats. Four years ago, Abe had felt dumbstruck when he first saw them, complete with seat backs. Vanessa had called them "butt savers." Americans could think of a million different ways to spend their money!

As the Central crew set up the hurdles, the starter tested his signal. Good, Abe observed, it's an air can, not a pistol. They usually used them for outdoor meets, but Abe wasn't complaining.

Abe was assigned lane three, reserved for the fastest runner. Central's best hurdler took lane four. Khalid was setting his blocks in lane one. Abe gave him a thumb's up sign and Khalid flashed his pearly whites. Cocky, Abe thought, as he settled into the starting blocks. Let him *prove* he is the best.

"Runners, take your mark," said the starter.

Abe raised his hips, ready to explode.

"BLARE!" And Abe bolted from the blocks and took

off too close to the first hurdle—that extra speed
and power from sprinting must have monkeyed with
his rhythm. He concentrated and regained his form:
one,two,three, snap, one,two,three, snap. Out of the
corner of his eyes, Abe didn't see the white uniforms
of the Central runners. He saw only the red of his
own school colors. Khalid was keeping it neck and
neck. The crowd was going wild! Over the fourth
hurdle, the finish line came into sight. Monica was
bouncing like a pogo stick beyond it, cheering for him.
He snapped out of the last hurdle and leaned into the
finish. But he didn't feel the tight spring across his
chest as usual. The officials compared their times—it
was a tie! With Khalid.

Abe spotted George and Vanessa, who were on their
feet, waving at him. George held up his finger and
shouted, "Number One!"

Well, Abe thought, he wasn't the only "number one."

Khalid spoke out of the corner of his mouth. "That's
first place for me, Liberian boy."

Monica ran over. "That was unconscious! Man, you
looked like a machine on overdrive."

"Was okay," Abe mumbled, grabbing his warm-ups.

Khalid passed by, saying, "Just don't blow the relay
later."

Abe's fists clenched as he stared at Khalid's back.

"Abe, let him be," Monica said, rubbing his hand.
"He thinks he's such a badass. When Tamika went
out with him, she said he looked at himself in the
mirror the whole time."

Abe took a deep breath. "You're right, he's not worth
my brain power."

A little while later, Monica's 60-meter race was up.
Abe was sitting between his parents. "Watch this,

George," Abe said. "She's like a tiger on the kill."

BLARE! The girls took off. "Dig, dig, dig," Abe cheered. He watched in amazement how every muscle in Monica's body was churning and pulsating. She was a blur of red and brown. Her skin was glistening, the gym lights flashing off—

> *the peoples' tear-stained faces, their sweat-coated arms and legs, "spray slightly ahead of them and watch them run into the bullets, the idiots," James was even laughing as he shot them, and the targets became a blur of brown, black and now... red,*

Abe hunched over squeezing his head between his hands. "Noooo," he muttered.

A hand landed on his back and he threw his elbow wildly to shuck it off. His elbow connected with something hard like bone. It felt good.

"Abe!" came a whisper—his mother? "Abe! Snap out of it!"

And the vision lifted as suddenly as it had shrouded him. Bent over, Abe started shaking and panting. Vanessa squeezed his spastic knee over and over. "Oh Abe, it's going to be all right," she soothed. They sat a while, Abe's wild breathing subsiding. No one had seemed to notice them—the races were too exciting.

After a few minutes, Vanessa gave Abe her handkerchief. He dried his eyes and blew his nose. He put his hand over his heart and took some deep breaths.

Vanessa spoke in a murmur. "The first few nights with us, you'd wake up crying. I'd rub your back and sing, 'Mocking Bird,' and you'd fall asleep. I felt proud—that I could take your hurt away for a while.

It's not so easy this time, Abe. It's so deep that I can't even reach it."

Abe nodded. It suddenly hit Abe that George wasn't next to him. "Where's George?" he mumbled.

"Honey, he got a bloody nose, so he went to the bathroom."

He locked onto her eyes and asked, "Did I do that? Tell me I didn't do that."

Vanessa pursed her lips.

Abe's ribs crushed his heart. "I need to see him."

Vanessa nodded in the direction of the hall.

Abe trotted off. Near the door, he glanced back. Vanessa was leaning over, massaging her brow as if she had a migraine headache.

Monica caught his eye and called, "Abe?"

"Later!" he told her, watching her eyebrows draw together in worry.

When Abe reached the men's room, he found George leaning over the sink, putting cold compresses on the bridge of his nose. Abe kicked a trash can over and almost put his fist through the condom machine.

"It's okay, Son. I know you didn't mean it."

Suddenly a toilet flushed and the stall door opened. Abe straightened up. It was Khalid, who did a second take when he saw the scene.

"Whassup, Abe?" Khalid asked, washing his hands at the far sink.

After he didn't get an answer, he added, "Whatever it is, you'd better get it all out of your system before the relay. The meet's gonna be tight right up to the end."

"I'll be fine," Abe barked.

After Khalid left, Abe hugged George from behind. "What did I do? I'm sorry, I don't know what happened, I'm so sorry."

For a few moments, he hung on George like a threadbare coat on a hook.

George turned Abe around and leaned him against the wall. Abe felt like he was in front of a firing squad, yet at the same time, he was part of the squad aiming for the kill.

"Do you want me to call Dr. Carlson?" George said.

"No, I'll be all right," Abe groaned.

George ignored him, got Carlson's number off his phone's memory, and punched in the number. Abe could hear the nasal voice of an answering service— thank God. George left a message, then put the phone away. "Carlson's out of town this weekend, Abe. Do you want to see the doctor who's covering for him?"

Abe shook his head.

"I didn't think so," George muttered. "Want to talk to me about it?"

Abe shrugged, then nodded. "Not here, though."

"Let's go home," George said, herding Abe toward the door.

"Wait." Abe walked back to the sink and washed his face with cold water. He placed some paper towels on his face and got himself together. "I'm going to stay," he told George. "They're counting on me for the relay."

"I knew you would say that," George said, shaking his head. "But you sit with us until your event, got it? If I spot anything strange, we're outta here."

Abe nodded. He sat with George and Vanessa, feeling safe between them and their "butt savers" seats. At one point, Monica motioned to him and mouthed, "Can we talk?" Abe pursed his lips and shook his head. Not a good idea. Abe didn't trust himself. Monica wrapped her arms around her waist and wandered to the other end of the gym.

As the meet progressed, Abe felt a little better. Something about watching Niko throw a 12-pound iron ball 42 feet made Abe feel in the here and now, in the absurd reality of sports.

A few minutes before his relay, Abe warmed up. Coach reminded him, "Stay in the hand-off zone, sync up with your team mates on each pass."

Abe nodded, visualizing himself with the baton. His eyes didn't stray to George or Vanessa; he didn't search for Monica. One thing at a time, he cautioned himself.

BLARE! The runners were off for the first hundred—two laps. His team got burned during the first leg the relay. Abe had to stand in the second lane over. The baton passed smoothly, and Abe dug in to make up the three meters between him and Central's sprinter ahead. He almost caught him at the end of his leg. Abe was so focused on the runner, though, he almost ran by his team mate at the hand-off. By the time Khalid got the baton two laps later, the race was even. On the curves, Khalid ran behind Central's guy, but on the home stretch, Khalid moved outside and opened up his stride. He blew into first, then raised his arms in triumph after he crossed the finish line.

The relay team crashed each other in joy—even Khalid got some of Abe's skin. Caught up in the absurd reality of winning a battle, Abe thrust his fist up. It met only air.

CHAPTER NINE

That night, Vanessa took in a movie with some friends, so the "boys" feasted on roast chicken from the market.

After he devoured both drumsticks and a pound of mashed potatoes, Niko said, "I got dibs on the shower, Abe. You hustle in after me, 'cause we should leave for the party around seven thirty."

"Uh, Nik, I'm not going tonight," Abe mumbled. "My head's killing me."

"Aw, c'mon. Monica's going to be there."

"Yeah, I know," Abe said, clearing the dishes. "I already called her. She understood." At least that was what she said. She sounded distant, as if she were calling from a pay phone on Mars.

"Abe—"

"Nik," George interrupted, "let it go."

Niko glanced back and forth at Abe and his father. "What's the word here? What're you keep'n from me?"

George cocked his head at Abe. "It's your call."

"Yeah, all right," Abe said. "Nik, I had another flashback today—at the meet. I remembered that my friends Steven and James actually killed people."

"Oh, shit," Niko whispered. "That makes two spells in three days."

"What?" asked George, hands on his hips.

"Oops," Nik said. "I'd better hit that shower."

Abe gritted his teeth. Niko had the mouth of a whale.

George pleaded, "Abe, you have to let us know when this stuff happens!" He eyed Abe, probably hoping for a reply, but Abe had none. George cleared his throat and said, "I'll give you five minutes to get your story together." He got up, made a pot of decaf, then took the trash out.

Abe wiped the table off and got out cups, cream and sugar. When the coffee machine finished, Abe poured two cups, leaving George's black. Abe stared down into his coffee. It was the color of a lake that had been rained upon for a week.

> *A muddy lake—the best time to get rid of bodies, we'll be long gone before anybody discovers the dead.*

After George returned, Abe explained how firing the laser gun triggered the flashback he'd had in front of Monica and Niko.

"Do you want to talk about the flashback itself? Or would you rather save this for Dr. Carlson?" George asked.

"I dunno. I got no problem talking about it. It's not like I did anything weird or wrong. It was James—"

"Is it James's voice you always hear in your flashbacks?"

"Mostly."

Abe couldn't stand how Steven's twin brother acted five years older. He always had the answers. James liked playing soldier with the guns because it made him feel more important—better than the rest of the prisoners.

"Grant, an officer, really liked James."

"Doesn't sound like *you* liked him."

"I hated James. He had no heart."

"Why do you say that?"

Abe pushed his chair back hard and the scraping sound made his shoulder muscles tighten. "George, this sitting here, it feels like an interrogation."

"I'm sorry," George said right away. "I must sound like a hypocrite. On one hand, making you see Dr. Carlson, and on the other hand, expecting you to spill your guts to me." George grimaced and massaged his brow. "My bad," he said.

"It's not that I *don't* want to talk to you. I do, but it's hard sitting here all comfy and picturing myself back there. Maybe going outside will help?"

"Sure," George replied. "We do good on walks."

On summer nights, the pleasure boats would twinkle on the bay's horizon like an endless necklace. Tonight, only the lonely buoy light blinked under the cloudy, moonless sky. Abe heard the water but he couldn't see it. The beach beneath their feet was swollen with melting snow. Good thing Abe had worn his boots. His feet sank so deep, it reminded him of the long forced march through swamplands.

Abe started speaking. "The rebels got word that the government forces were closing in on our college camp. We had to leave fast. But the rebels didn't want to bring everybody because it would have taken too long. We wouldn't have moved fast enough."

George asked, "Did they free everyone?"

For all his book knowledge, George could be pretty naïve or ignorant or both sometimes. "No," Abe replied. "They shot everyone who wasn't useful—sick people, old ones."

"Of course," George mumbled, hitting the side of his head. "I'd heard stuff like that in the refugee camp. I guess I didn't want to believe it."

"Seeing is believing," Abe answered. "Anyway, they brought a lot of girls and women—my mom, Ellie and about thirty others. When it was time to leave, they gave some of us boys our own guns, and ordered us to use them against the enemy."

"They actually armed you—with ammo?"

"Yeah."

Abe bowed his head. The image of his mother came back to him. When the soldiers had shoved the women into the rain, Abe couldn't pick her out at first. All the women looked ragged, stony, caved-in under their cheekbones. The rebels had worked them hard but gave them little food. Suddenly he saw a woman's mouth gape open. It was his mother. Her eyes filled, but they didn't spill over.

"I can't believe it," she had said, spitting at Abe's feet. "Now you're one of them."

He had said, "No, I—"

Ellie had caught up, narrowing her eyes with disgust at Abe. She shook Bunny at him, working its mouth. It said, "You stink!" Then she pulled their mother away.

"Abe?" George asked, with a nudge.

"Oh yeah."

"So your mother and sister were okay at that point," George stated.

Okay? What did "okay" mean? Abe couldn't find the words to explain, so he simply nodded.

Abe jammed his fists into his pockets and picked up the thread of the story. "We'd been on the road to Monrovia for a couple of hours when we were told to jump into the forest and hide. We were going to ambush some troops heading our way in vehicles. My mom and the others ran deep into the forest, and we hung back off the road just a few yards.

"Grant had given us what he called nose candy—"

"Coke?" George interrupted.

"Something more like meth. It was easier to make," Abe said. "There were plenty of chemicals at the college, and later, even more at the factory. Plus they must have looted a dozen pharmacies, clinics, doctors' offices."

"Oh my God," George said, his hand squeezing his brow. "When I first noticed you in the camp, you had chills and you looked feverish. Malaria? I'd wondered, but you wouldn't let me touch you or bring you into the clinic, and you wouldn't follow me. Drugs? You were thirteen! You were probably going through withdrawal. How stupid of me!"

Withdrawal—that's what it was? Abe remembered how everything hurt after he'd escaped from the rebels. It felt as if he were being squeezed by a giant vice. Stifled with fever one moment, and wracked with chills the next. A terrible craving twisted his mind. He would have done anything for more of Grant's white magic. After about ten days, it suddenly stopped. Withdrawal. He'd never go through that again. No matter how good some guy said Ecstasy or Oxy-Contin was, Abe would never touch a drug again.

"So, we're on the road to Monrovia," Abe continued.

"Remember Grant? He told us, 'On my signal, jump out first and start firing.' Steven asked him, 'Why do we have to go first? We're just learning how to shoot.' Grant said, 'Since you're so little, you make a bad target. Besides, they don't want to kill kids, they want to kill us men.'"

Abe paused. He stared out at the black water, hoping it would wash away all of his memories some day.

After a minute of silence, George asked, "Do you want to tell me about it?"

Abe clenched his fists with a familiar craving.

"I know it's hard, Abe," George said, clutching Abe's upper arms. "You can save it for Dr. Carlson, if you want—."

"No, I don't want to save it. Don't you see? I don't want it in my head anymore. Here's what happened: The convoy got even with us, Grant signaled, and Steven jumped up and sprayed bullets all over the place. He was the only person out there—nobody backed him up, not even me! Suddenly Steven's body started jerking, blood shooting everywhere. Then James jumped out—still nobody else had, no men— and James shot everybody, I mean everybody! Turns out the 'convoy' was only two escort cars, one in the front and one way back."

George, panting, said, "What do you mean 'escort'? Escorting who? An official?"

"They were refugees, man! Refugees or prisoners like us—I don't know who, or from where, but it didn't matter anymore! James mowed them down, kids, grannies, all of them, and the rear escort turned around and drove away, leaving everybody there to die."

Abe dropped to his knees and hunched over. Bitter

coffee regurgitated and choked him. He couldn't get his breath through his sobs.

George knelt alongside Abe and put his arm around him. "It's okay, it's out now. It's okay," he murmured.

Once he could breathe better, Abe moaned, "Steven was all chewed up by bullets. His face was gone, his arm was sitting ten feet away."

Abe's voice turned bitter. "And you asked about James's heart? Well, James didn't even cry, and he didn't even help bury Steven. Grant came up and said, 'Good work, James!' And gave him some pills. Then Grant and another guy buried Steven on the side of the road. They didn't bother with the refugees. 'Leave them as a sign,' Grant had said."

George leaned back and gazed into Abe's eyes. "I wish I had something to tell you, Abe, something to make it all go away. I'm sorry you had to go through such a horror. No one—especially a child—should have to experience that."

Abe felt exhausted, as if he'd run three miles of hurdles. George pulled out his cell phone and dialed home. "Nik, oh, good, you're still home. Come get Abe and me. We'll meet you at the beach parking lot."

Abe looked up. It was only thirty yards away. He could make it physically. Mentally, he wasn't sure.

Despite his fatigue, Abe couldn't sleep that night. His legs felt as if electrical currents were running through them. And he couldn't get his mind off Liberia. More shooting rang in his ears, more trudging and hiding. And more distance between him and his mother and Ellie. They wouldn't even look at him.

Abe's mind returned to James. From that point on,

he was like the rebels' mascot. Grant had given him a camouflage outfit with the sleeves and pants cut to fit. They let him hang around and drink all the palm wine he wanted. And he let them do anything they wanted with him. He loved them. James didn't have Steven anymore. The rebels became his family. Where was James now? Lying low, regaining strength, so to fight again with all the other maniacs?

It seemed as soon as Abe found sleep, the aroma of pancakes and sausage woke him up. He couldn't fight it, not on a Sunday morning.

Down in the kitchen, George hugged him tight. Then he served up some breakfast for them both. "Eat, chill out. The English muffins will pop in a sec."

"Thanks," Abe muttered.

They ate in silence a while—the food acting as an excuse not to talk. As soon as Abe's mouth was empty, he'd fill it again. He cleaned up his mess before heading out to the library.

"Abe, wait," George said.

Abe, silent, leaned against the door jam.

"I don't want to drag you through all that muck again. But whatever happened to James? Did he die too?"

Abe shrugged. "I figure, the way I'm hearing him, that he's still alive. He's a survivor type. I don't believe in stuff like haunting and communicating with the dead. I never hear Steven, or my mom, or Ellie. But James, yeah, he must still be out there somewhere. I've been hearing him a lot."

George nodded, his mouth full. Then he held up his hand to keep Abe from leaving the room again. "Hmmm," he said, swallowing. "Abe, I share everything with Vanessa. We don't keep secrets from each other. Is it okay for me to tell her about this?"

Abe thought a second. "Won't Vanessa freak out?"

"You know how strong she is, Abe. She gets all kinds of whacked cases down at her office. The more she knows about what *you've* been through, the better she'll understand you. I'll keep trying Dr. Carlson, so I can let him know what's been happening."

"I don't get it," Abe said, putting his hands on his hips. "If you all are going to know everything anyway, why do I have to see Dr. Carlson? Why don't I just put everything down in my journal, and you can read it whenever you want?"

"We're not psychiatrists—we don't have Carlson's knowledge and experience to deal with what's coming out of you. And I don't think any of us—including you—will ever know everything about what went down in Liberia."

CHAPTER TEN

Abe was bench-pressing 180 on the Bow-Flex when Niko straggled into the rec room around two o'clock. Niko grabbed a Pepsi from the fridge, flopped on the couch, and chugged the soda.

"Must have been a good party last night, huh, Nik?"

Niko belched in reply. "Hey, get me that bottle of Motrin."

"Get it yourself," Abe puffed as he pushed the weight up.

After he finished his tenth rep, Abe said, "You didn't drive home, did you?"

"No way, Leisha did. Can you drive me over to Vernon Heights to get my car?"

"No."

"What? How come?"

"Number one, even if I wanted to do you the favor, I can't. No driving, remember?" Abe said, wiping down his sweaty arms with a towel. "Number two, I don't *want* to because that would be letting you off too easy for drinking."

"Sheeeet," Niko said.

"Ride your bike."

"A senior stud like me riding a bike? Get out! I'll call Ray for a ride."

Niko flipped open his cell phone and had to leave a message. He tried another guy and got the same result.

Abe began squats with hundred pounds. "What if this happened every day?"

Niko gave him a blank look. "What do you mean 'this'?"

"That I can't drive and you can't drive."

Niko swatted away the words in the air. "'This' ain't going to happen again. I'm getting my car back one way or another any minute. And besides, you'll be fine soon."

Abe didn't know about that. "Nik, I don't want to sound like a preacher, but those rebels—most of them were all right to us when they were sober. But after drinking and snorting, they became monsters. If they had no one to fight, they'd fight each other, even killing each other."

Niko crushed his soda can against his head, then tossed it toward the waste basket. It missed, and he didn't get up to put it in. Abe let it slide.

"Abe, don't worry about me, okay? I'm not the fighting type, unless it's on a soccer field."

Abe stood and his anger rose as well. "Listen, I can't tip-toe around this problem anymore. I've seen you at parties—why do you think I insist on driving home after every one? You get smashed! You get caught DUI, you automatically lose your license for six months. I bet last night, you had to be pulled out of the driver's seat, so somebody else could drive you home."

Niko chuckled. "It took *three* guys to pull me out.

If it were some hag driving me home, they'd need ten guys. But you know how I feel about Leisha."

"This isn't funny!" Abe yelled. The anger burst, and Abe whirled and punched the wall.

Niko clammed right up.

Abe got in Niko's face so there was no air, no space for his words to wander. "You drive drunk and you become a killer. Same shit in Liberia. I've seen it. A few drinks, a couple of snorts—and all you need is a weapon."

"Whoa! Easy, Bro," said Niko leaning back.

A moment later a knock came at the door. Vanessa called, "Is everything all right in there. May I come in?"

Niko whispered, "Abe, man, don't tell her! I swear it'll never happen again."

Abe couldn't meet Niko's eyes. He stood up straight and grabbed a dumbbell.

"Yeah, Mom, come on in," Niko said cheerfully.

"I heard a noise. Did something hap—?" Vanessa gave a little gasp, and walked over to the punctured plaster on the wall. "What happened? Did either of you get hurt?"

"Sorry, Vanessa, it was my bad," Abe said. "I didn't put this dumbbell on tight enough, and it flew off when the barbell tipped."

"Good thing it didn't land on somebody's toes!" She ran her hand over the busted drywall. "I don't think your father can fix this. He can patch bodies, but he's not too handy at house repair."

"I just got a new poster!" Niko chipped in. "I'll put it right over the crack, and nobody will ever know the difference."

That was Niko, taking the easy way out. Still, Abe

loved him. He'd already lost his sister and mother. He couldn't take losing Niko, too.

Monday evening, George dropped Abe off for therapy. "Listen," George said, "This morning, I updated Carlson on your latest flashbacks and memories. So you don't have to repeat stuff."

"Thanks, I guess."

"Niko will pick you up in an hour," George added before driving away.

Dr. Carlson led Abe downstairs to the pool table again. They decided to play 8-ball this time. Abe broke and sank a low ball. He sank the 3 next, but missed on the 5.

As Dr. Carlson walked around the table to choose his next shot, he said, "Let's move forward, Abe, from Steven's death. Remember, I wanted you to talk about your mother and sister more. They survived the attack, I suppose?"

"Yeah, the rebels reassembled us, and we marched on. My mother and Ellie and the other women were all complaining of mosquito bites they got in the forest. I could barely see Ellie's left eye because the area around it had swelled up like donut. My mother still wouldn't look at me."

Dr. Carlson called a combo for his 13 ball and made it. Then he banked in the 10.

"When was the next time you spoke with them?"

"A few days later. The government forces were holding the Atlantic coast. So we swung east of Monrovia to come in from the northeast. The rebels spread a map on the ground. I learned we were meeting another group there—of the Khran tribe—and invading together."

"And Ellie and your mother?"

Abe cut the 2 ball into the side, and lined up a bridge shot—the 5 into the corner. He sank it. As he was placing the bridge back on the rack, he said, "You know, some stupid guys call this cue a 'sissy stick?'"

Dr. Carlson smiled. "Yes, I've heard that before. But I'd rather sink a ball using the bridge, than miss it by leaning so far you lose your balance."

Balance. That was a good word, a useful word. Nothing in Abe's past had been balanced. Especially after Steven died. Abe felt as though half his self had been hacked away.

And James didn't help at all after that. Whenever there was work to be done, he disappeared. While they were slashing their way around Monrovia, Abe had prisoners to prod, and firearms to clean. The responsibility intensified once they met up with the Khran, and struck camp in a deserted rubber factory.

Grant had told Abe, "We're going to be in meetings with the Khran leaders into the night. I want you to organize the kids to deliver meals to us officers first, then to the troops. Can you do that?"

"Yeah."

"That's my little soldier. I'll bring you a surprise later," he said, stroking Abe's cheek.

Abe had turned away before Grant could see the nausea on his face.

Startled by Dr. Carlson's touch, Abe jumped.

"Are you okay, Abe?"

"Uh, yeah."

"You were far away, there. Where exactly...with your mother?"

"Um, not really. Well, kind of. We camped in a factory," Abe said. "The women had carried the plates and pots from the college, and they set up a kitchen on the main factory floor. The leaders met in a large balcony office looking over the floor. Squads of soldiers surrounded the factory and kept guard. I saw Ellie and my mother a lot that first day. I was in charge of the food delivery."

"Did they acknowledge you? With a wave or smile?"

"My mom didn't look once, but Ellie stuck her tongue out at me."

"How did those reactions make you feel?"

"Worthless. Weak." Abe gazed down for a moment. "Lonely," he added, his voice broken up. "I didn't have anybody anymore."

Dr. Carlson said, "I know how painful that is. One by one friends in my squad were dying. I felt helpless to stop it. Sometimes I wished I'd be killed so I wouldn't have to face any more loss."

Abe looked up in anguish. "That's right. That's exactly how I felt. You know, nobody understands that. Niko, he pisses me off. He acts like there's nothing to lose. He has no clue what his death would do to the people who love him. Vanessa would fall to pieces! George would dive into work, pretending that nothing has changed. He'd be trying to buck everybody up, to care for everybody else but himself. And me? If Niko died?" Abe swung the cue over the table, gritting his teeth. "I'd want to kill someone."

"You'd want to *kill* someone?" Gently, Dr. Carlson took the cue from Abe, and guided him to a stool. "Why, Abe? Why would death make you want more death?"

"I don't know. I'd be mad. I'd want to use death, I guess, like a tool. I'd have the power. I could do something about whether someone lived or died." Abe hung his head. "That's messed up, isn't it, Dr. Carlson?"

"Actually," he admitted. "When you're surrounded by death, especially violent death, you want control over the situation. Is that how you felt?"

Abe nodded.

"Okay, now try to understand. That violence is all in your past. You're not surrounded by death anymore. I read in your journal that you're scared you might hurt people. You don't want to. That's good! There's no *cause* to have that ultimate power. There's no *need* to hurt anybody, especially your new family. You're surrounded by love now."

"I am?" Abe whispered with a sniffle. I am, he realized. But would it always be there?

They took a few moments to put the pool cues away, and cover the table. The doctor pointed at the stool again, and Abe obeyed.

"We have about twenty minutes left," Dr. Carlson said, "and I'd like to stick with the topic of family. Because you know your mother and Ellie still loved you, even though they might have been mad at you at that time."

Abe said, "I *didn't* know that then. That was the problem."

"Well, they did love you, Abe. Go on."

"That night, after all the kids had brought back the dinner plates, I helped them deliver flattened boxes that were found in the shipping department. The rebels used these as beds. There were many left, so the officers said the women could have them too. They would sleep right on that main floor, in view from the balcony. As I passed out the cardboard, I tried to talk to my mother. I really needed to be with her. I needed her to understand that I wasn't falling in with the soldiers. That I was just trying to do what I was told, to stay alive."

"Did you get to her?"

"Yes, I was on my way when I saw Ellie and my mother creep along the outside wall. I was shocked. I whispered, 'Mom! What are you doing?'

"She put her finger to her lips and shushed me. She said, 'I know this area. I have an old friend here. We're going to her house. Come with us!'

"'The rebels will kill us if they catch us! They're monsters.'

"'The rebels are already killing us, day in and day out!' my mother argued. 'If you don't want to come right now with us, help us at least.'

"I glanced around and saw an armed guard about twenty yards away. 'I'll try to distract that guard over there,' I told them. 'When I wave my hand behind me, sprint for those woods.'

"'Thank you, Son,' my mother said. 'Take this address—I know it by heart.'

"'Maybe I could join you in a day or two?'

"'Please try,' Ellie replied. 'I need to play soccer with someone.'"

Abe's brow relaxed. "Maybe you're right, Dr. Carlson. Maybe they didn't hate me."

Dr. Carlson smiled. "Go on."

"I approached the soldier closest to my mother's escape route. Another twenty yards away, the rebels were busy washing up a bit, or talking—cigarettes glowing—in small circles.

"I approached the guard, who jumped up and put a gun on me. The whites of his eyes blazed into mine. I put my hands in the air. 'Wait! I come from the officers,' I said. 'To see if you need anything.'

"The man lowered his gun, and took a seat on a tree stump. I positioned myself to block the guard's vision. 'Tell the Gio officers that we never got the grenade launchers they promised to us.'

"'Okay,' I said, waving behind my back. I wanted to give Ellie and Mom more time to get away, so I asked the soldier a few questions about where he lived. He was sixteen, and played forward in soccer too. After about eight or ten minutes, I told the soldier I'd deliver his message. I turned toward the main building, and suddenly shots rang out nearby. Rebel guards jumped up, fumbling for their guns.

"And I heard my mother and sister screaming!

"Is that how they died?" Dr. Carlson asked. "Trying to escape?"

Abe lifted his head, tears teetering. "It must be."

"I'm so sorry, Abe. It's horrible and it's so unfair." The doctor held Abe as he shuddered and cried. After a few minutes, he held Abe's shoulders and looked up into his eyes. "Abe, that's enough for tonight. We made real good progress. We now know how your mother and sister died—"

"That's 'real good progress?'"

"Yes!" Dr. Carlson said, giving Abe a little shake. "They and you were acting—not reacting. You three were taking steps to become a family again. You helped them, and they let you know they wanted you. See? Even when you all were surrounded by death, there was love among you. Do you understand?"

"I think so." Abe blew out a huge breath and wiped his face. His eyes had swollen almost shut.

Outside, Niko was waiting in the driveway. No alcohol on his breath. No shorties in the car. No wise cracks. Abe let him babble the whole way home.

CHAPTER ELEVEN

Tuesday, Abe and Monica spent their free period in the library, quizzing each other for their history exam.

Monica asked, "Where did Robert E. Lee surrender to Grant?"

Grant. That name again. That face—would he ever forget it? Grant had a poorly healed scar on his chin beneath a set of disgusting teeth every color in the rainbow. And he inflicted them on everyone by smiling all the time—probably because he was stoned. His round face matched his round body. For a rebel, he certainly ate very well. He had a bulbous nose and bushy eyebrows. And his eyes were crazy. You couldn't even say he had whites around his pupils. The red veins formed a cluttered map, with all roads leading to his dark vision.

Monica's voice broke in: "Abe—you there?"

Abe blinked. "Sorry."

"You'd better not zone out like that during the test. You'll flunk."

"And that's the last thing I'd want to do, with Blalock head of the history department."

"Appomattox," Monica said.

"What?"

"That's where Lee surrendered. Remember!"

Monica closed her book and rested her chin on her hand. "Where did you go that time, just now?"

"The name, Grant. That was the name of one of the rebel officers in Liberia."

"The one who gave you boys gifts and special treatment?"

Abe chuckled at the thought of Grant's version of special treatment. In the beginning, Grant would send Steven and him a bit ahead of the unit to "explore." It took the boys a while to figure out that Grant was testing the road or a field for land mines. It hit home when a kid blew up right in front of their eyes. Abe and the other older boys then refused to do it. So Grant started giving out candy to five- and six-year-olds to do it. He told them, "I'm giving you twenty minutes of free time. Go play in that field." The kids didn't know any better. And us big boys were not allowed to tell them.

Abe caught motion in front of his eyes. Monica had been waving her hand at his face. "Abe, how come you're remembering all this stuff now? Like, haven't you ever thought about it over the past four years?"

Abe leaned back and sneered "You my new doctor or something?"

"No—I—"

"Monica, I'm being poked all over by so many different people. I don't need you—the journalist—'interviewing' me."

"I thought we were having a conversation." Monica stood abruptly. "Well, don't worry. I'll think twice before I talk to you again."

Watching Monica bolt out of the library, Abe felt a sudden, inexplicable relief.

When Abe arrived for his appointment Wednesday evening, Dr. Carlson didn't offer him any food or a game of pool. He was all business. He led Abe into an office and pointed to a brown leather Lazy-boy.

"Make yourself comfortable," he said. "Beats a couch, huh?"

Abe stretched out, his size 14 feet flopping off the footrest.

Dr. Carlson pulled up a desk chair alongside Abe, facing him. "I'd like to try something with you that's worked really well on other patients who have been in war zones."

Abe folded his arms. "Gonna hypnotize me or something?"

"Something like that. How did you guess?"

"Niko guessed it. And I don't want to do it," Abe stated. "Last year a hypnotist gave a school assembly, and he hypnotized these kids. He made them do a lot of stupid things, like stand on their heads. I'm not going to make a fool of myself."

"Don't worry," Dr. Carlson said. "Nobody is here to laugh at you. Besides, you won't do anything that, deep down, you don't want to. I will make sure you're safe at all times. And remember, anything you say or do with me stays private. I won't even tell your parents if you don't want me to."

Abe ground his teeth. "I still don't know why you want to keep doing this. What do you think you're going to learn?"

Dr. Carlson rolled his seat over to a filing cabinet,

and pulled out an article. "Read this, Abe," he said, rolling back. "I'll give you a minute." Then he left the room.

*Repressed Traumas Revealed Through
Hypnotism: Veterans Purge and Heal*

Abe read that a hypnotic state provided a safe place for people to bring out their most painful memories—memories that might destroy them if they were fully conscious. I don't have anything *that* bad, Abe figured. I've already told George the worst of it. So, then, I've got nothing to lose with hypnosis, right? Abe read the rest of the article, relaxing. It didn't seem like he was going to look stupid.

When Dr. Carlson returned, Abe tried to hand the article back. "No, you keep it, Abe. I have lots of copies. So... are you ready?"

"Yeah," Abe said. "Sounds okay."

"Exactly. Now I'm going to make you fall into a sleep-like trance. You will wake up when I say...um, 'hurdles,' okay? So close your eyes and focus on my voice. It's like a lullaby your mother sang to you when you were a little boy, soft and low, with sweet sounds, a lullaby full of magical words and soft melodies, over and over she'd sing it, softly low and sweet...."

Totally relaxed, Abe nodded when the Doctor asked, "Can you hear me?"

Dr. Carlson said, "You're back in Liberia now, Abe. You and Steven and James are playing with guns, but they don't have any ammunition in them. What games did you play?"

Abe pictured his best friend Steven hiding behind a tree. Abe saw himself inching up behind him, lips tight trying not to laugh and give himself away. "Capture, we'd play capture," he told Dr. Carlson. "Like chase or hide and seek. I always won—Steven was chubby and his butt or his belly would give him away. He'd take so long to find me that sometimes I'd stick my foot out for him to see."

"You were good at hiding?" Dr. Carlson asked.

"Yeah."

"How about James? Was he good at hiding?"

"No, yes, I don't remember."

"Did you hide at other times? When you weren't playing around?"

"At night."

"At night, yes. Why did you hide at night?"

"Grant wanted to play."

"But you boys liked Grant. He gave you special treats. He gave you the guns. Why would you hide from him?"

"He made us play with other soldiers too. He gave us banana rum and palm wine, and he liked to watch us."

"How did that make you feel?"

"I was mad, but I was more afraid of what would happen to me if I didn't do what Grant and the other guys told me to do."

"Like *what* would happen?"

"Grant said he'd hurt Mommy and Ellie."

"Oh.... Before Steven died, was he with you those times?"

"Yes, it was harder for Steven. The drinks and drugs made him puke."

"And James?"

"He liked the drugs."

"Tell me about James. Was he tall?"

"Uhh, yeah, about my size."

"Thin?"

"Yeah, but with muscles. He was stronger than me and Steven put together."

"How would I choose him out of a crowd? Did he have any special mark—a birth mark or a tattoo?"

"He had two scars, but you couldn't see them."

"Could you show me where?"

"I don't want to."

"Okay, Abe. Just point to the places. You don't have to take any clothes off."

"I don't know."

"Abe, remember that I'm a doctor who's trying to help you. I would never hurt you."

"Okay. One's down here, near my crotch. The other is over on the behind."

Dr. Carlson paused to jot a few notes. "Abe, do you know how James got scars there? Did a bullet hit him?"

"No. There was a knife and it slipped."

"Did James tell you that?"

"Grant did."

"What? James wasn't alone when it happened?"

"No, Grant was there."

"Was Grant holding the knife when it slipped?"

"No, somebody else."

"Did it hurt James?"

"Yeah, a lot. But it hurt worse when Grant started fixing it. He poured a drink on it to clean it. It stung so bad. Then he squeezed the gash closed to stop the bleeding. Other soldiers gave me more rum so I would stop crying, then they held me down while Grant sewed up the gash. It still hurt for days and days. I felt torn into pieces. But after a while, I figured that the pain was worth it.

"How could that be?" Dr. Carlson asked.

"Because after that Grant left me alone at night and he didn't let the other soldiers play with me and I didn't have to hide anymore. But Steven...Steven...."

"So you're sure this happened *before* Steven died?"

"Yes, yes, about two weeks before the ambush. I think...I think Steven wanted to die, and I wanted to die with him. So when Steven fell over, I jumped up too and shot and shot and shot. The stupid escort car turned around, and nobody else in the convoy had guns. I didn't know that! I didn't know right away that the only other person shooting was...me."

"You said 'me' and 'I.' Is James talking right now?"

"No, I'm Abe."

"Where is James?"

"He's inside me."

"Is he real? Is he alive?"

"He's real. But how can he be alive? He doesn't have a heart."

"Okay, all right. But how can I know he's inside you."

"I'll show you."

"Show me? How?"

"I'll show you my scars."

CHAPTER TWELVE

"Hurdles!"

Abe found himself sitting up straight in the recliner. His belt buckle was loose. Gripping the arms of the chair, he felt petrified. His ribcage weighed a thousand pounds, crushing his breath and heartbeat. He stared into Dr. Carlson's concerned eyes.

The doctor squeezed Abe's hand. "It's all right."

It could never be all right, Abe knew. It *was* all right, once—a lifetime ago—for Steven and him, his mom and Ellie. But it could never be right again. Words came out between his gritted teeth: "I killed people? *I* did it?"

"Abe, listen. It's not your fault," Dr. Carlson assured him.

"I pulled the trigger. I killed. My mother was right. I *was* one of them. There was no stupid 'James.'"

"There *was*, Abe. That's just it! In your mind, James came to life. The term is called 'dissociation.'"

"I don't care what it's called! I killed innocent people!"

"Please listen, Abe," Dr. Carlson implored. "Just hear me out. James did all the things that Abe knew a person shouldn't do. All those things that the soldiers did, they did to James. James didn't have a heart to break. You needed James, so that Abe could live!"

"I don't want to live! I don't deserve to live!—"

"Now, Abe," Dr. Carlson began, reaching for Abe's hand, "You—"

"I'm scared."

"Yes, I can understand that. What scares you the most?"

Abe's lips quivered. "I've been shaky in the last few weeks. I wanted to hit things, people. I *did* hit them. Where's James now?"

Dr. Carlson took a deep breath, then said, "You and I are going to do everything we can to get rid of him for good."

"Is he still inside me? Is he coming back? I'm scared to be alone. I shouldn't be near anybody. But I'm scared to be alone."

"I'm not going to let you be alone." Dr. Carlson wheeled over to his desk and made a phone call.

Abe tried to stand up and stretch. He felt dizzy on his feet and leaned on a window sill for balance. He opened the window and took in the cold damp air. He didn't want to think but his mind pummeled him with questions: Will I go to jail? Could I be tried for war crimes? Murder? How many counts, my God—they're not fucking numbers—how many *people* have I killed? Did I kill again? Did I do any other horrible things I'd seen the rebels do—torture? Arson? Rape?

"Abe?" Dr. Carlson cleared his throat. "I just tried to get you a bed in Green Lake, but there won't be one available until Friday morning."

Green Lake? The psycho ward? Abe's mouth dropped open. A bed? A room? No way! He had been down those halls. When he had first come to America, he had met with Dr. Carlson in his office there, and attended some group therapy. It had always seemed like a prison, with its locks, wired glass, and warning systems. He only felt liberated once he'd walk back out and breathed fresh air, uncontaminated air.

"Dr. Carlson, I can't go there to stay," Abe pleaded. "I don't want to be locked up—I'm done being locked up."

"Abe, you're going to need supervision, intensive therapy and powerful medicine to help you get through this.... Now, we need to meet with your parents."

"I thought everything was confidential! I can't let them know that I've k—, k—, that I was a soldier."

"Don't worry, Abe. We don't have to tell them everything. But I have some ideas about how to treat you, and I'd like to go over the choices all together."

A few moments later, Dr. Carlson was arranging a 5 pm meeting for the next day in his office. He covered the mouthpiece and asked Abe, "Do you want Niko to attend the meeting?"

Abe nodded immediately, knowing he'd need a crutch. Niko would probably think it was cool to shoot live ammo, real people. Abe heard Dr. Carlson quietly talking to Vanessa. "Oh, George is on call at the hospital tonight? Well, then, can you come pick up Abe? He can't be left alone." A pause, an overflowing silence, filled the room. Dr. Carlson met Abe's eyes and added, "We've had a major breakthrough. I'll give you instructions when you come."

In Dr. Carlson's presence, Vanessa stood firm and resolute. He told her that Abe had been more involved in fighting than they'd thought.

"I'll do anything to help Abe get through his troubles. I'll take tomorrow and Friday off," she said, "And I'll notify the school." But on the way home, Vanessa chatted nervously about everything *but* Abe. She'd attended a conference today in Annapolis. "It kills me! The State cuts our funding, then wonders how social work clients keep falling through the cracks...."

Usually, Abe liked to talk with Vanessa about her work. It amazed him that so many people in America had jobs to simply help those in need. The only place Abe had seen that was in the refugee camp. But this evening, her words seeped far and farther away.

Abe had counted four bridges so far between Dr. Carlson's and their home. Lots of inlets and small rivers shared the tide with the bay. East, the Bay Bridge arched over the water like an angel, its wings stretching skyward, lights twinkling like sequins of heavenly grace.

Now that would be some jump, Abe pictured. And at this point in the winter, the water would instantly freeze the life out of him. Abe saw himself plummeting headfirst like a kingfisher after a crab. He would want to feel the crash of his body against the water. He deserved to feel pain like the people he shot. He needed to die a slow death, to sink, drinking his last breath, a rush of salty liquid. His last vision, an angel of forgiveness.

Here was another bridge! Not a quarter as high as the Bay Bridge, but it would do. For repentance. He couldn't take living anymore, because he had already taken so many other lives. He didn't deserve to have a wonderful family, his brains, his abilities, a chance to go to college. In a split second, he unbuckled himself and yanked the door handle.

"Abe, noooo!" Vanessa cried.

But Abe had already opened the door and dived out. His head clanged against a guardrail, his body whipping across the gravel shoulder. He felt himself falling and falling faster. Abruptly, pain careered through his head, and spread downward. He was rolling down a steep bank, his clothing dampening. Then he was totally soaked, face down in shallow water. It wouldn't take long....

Distorted words reached his water-filled ears. "Abe? Where are you? Abe?" Vanessa screeching.

"Abe!" She shrieked, and she rolled him over.

Abe squinted away from the glare of her flashlight. "Abe, honey! What did you do? Oh Abe."

Forehead splitting and bleeding into his eyes, Abe felt himself dragged up the bank. Everything ached the way he'd hoped. His head hammered. Fiery stabs riddled his neck. When he coughed, his throat felt ragged. His ribs crumpled on his right side. He could tell he was bleeding inside his abdomen. It felt pulpy.

Vanessa cried into her cell phone: "I've got an emergency!"

Shit, Abe thought. He was alive and people were trying to keep him that way.

"Can you open your eyes again, honey?" Vanessa asked, squeezing his hand. "There...there you go."

Abe tried to sit up but he had no stomach strength, only ripping pain. "You're in ICU, Abe," Vanessa informed him. "You had an accident last night. Do you remember?"

He nodded slightly.

"It's Thursday night, now. I'm so glad you're alive,"

she choked out.

She'd been crying. She looked a mess. She probably blamed herself for Abe's action. Now he was causing *her* pain. He was still causing pain to people he loved. His breath caught. It hurt. Good. Maybe he'd punctured his lungs and crushed an artery.

"Niko's here. See?" she said.

Niko's bottom lip trembled like he was going to bawl. But he forced a smile and said, "Hey, my African brother. Welcome back to the world."

That was about the worst thing Niko could say right now. But that was Niko.

"I got a laundry list of what you did to yourself. Want to hear it?"

Niko was going to tell him anyway, so Abe acted interested with a small nod.

"Three broken ribs on your right side, two others only fractured. Collapsed lung on that side. Torn diaphragm. Bruised liver. The surgeon said you were lucky you didn't land on your left side, because, you know, the heart and your spleen. I told the doctor, 'Lucky Abe's a lefty too!'"

Abe blinked. Lucky me.

Niko read from the chart again. "Fractured right collarbone, fractured right cheekbone, fractured skull. Plus on your arms and legs, a mess of hematomas, um, hematomi?"

Vanessa piped in, "That's just a fancy name for a deep bruise."

Niko pointed to all the tubes and meters, and spouted them off like they were specials in a restaurant. "You got your heart monitor, you got your blood pressure, you got your oxygen, your IV full of saline solution and whatever legal drugs they're piping into you.

And here you got some bags of...um, how should I say this delicately with a lady in the room? Bags of *output*."

Abe winced. So now the whole world can literally see my shit.

Vanessa handed him a cup of shaved ice. After a few mouthfuls, Abe said, "I'm sorry." For living, he wanted to add, but they wouldn't have liked that.

Niko's lip was at it again. He fumbled for words, "Why did you do, it, Abe? What could be so bad that you'd want to k—, hurt yourself?"

Abe squeezed his eyes shut, tears pooling near the bridge of his nose.

Vanessa said, "Shhh, honey. Now that you're out of danger, we have plenty of time to talk. We'll let you rest. George is on the overnight shift and will visit you. And we'll see you tomorrow."

She kissed him good-bye on his left cheek. Niko waved. "Hang in there, dog."

Sometime in the middle of the night, Abe sensed a quiet presence nearby. It certainly wasn't a nurse; they clanged and banged and bumped around. He opened his eyes to find George at the foot of the bed. George smiled and shuffled to the bed side. He ran the back of his hand down Abe's left cheek.

"I'm so sorry," George said. "I'm the one who's pushing all this on you. It's too much to handle all at once. I should have figured things out sooner. I should have understood right from the start the magnitude of what you'd been through. I guess I felt that adopting you, taking you far away from the war, was enough. Obviously, I was very very wrong."

Abe licked his lips. "Did Carlson tell you about last night?"

"No, he didn't give any details beyond your involve-

ment in fighting. But he said you need more help, serious help, twenty-four seven. We'll get together soon,
maybe tomorrow, when you're feeling up to it, Abe.
Until then, you're to have around-the-clock care and
supervision." George lowered his voice and added,
"You're on suicide watch."

It would be hard to kill himself now. He was so
sore, and exhausted with agony. Plus he was all
wrapped up like a mummy. When a nurse came in,
George kissed Abe good-bye "for now." The nurse gave
him a dose of something through his IV port and laid
a warmed blanket over him. He fell deeply asleep for
the first time in months. His body had healing to do,
and left no energy for his brain to conjure ghosts.

CHAPTER THIRTEEN

Friday night, Abe spotted a bundle of smile-face balloons bouncing to the ICU nurse's station. A nurse
took them, and a disappointed Monica and Jermaine
appeared. Monica's face slackened when she came to
the doorway and caught sight of Abe. But she bravely
worked up a smile.

"The nurse said no balloons in the ICU rooms,"
Monica explained. "It was weird—she'd said, 'the he-
lium balloons are dangerous, especially the strings.'
Give me a break—the strings? She let me bring a
card, at least. Better watch out. It might give you a
paper cut."

Abe took it and said to Jermaine, "Hey, little man."

"Can I try on your hat?" asked Jermaine, climbing
onto the bed.

"No honey!" Monica scolded and swooped him
into her arms before he could cause Abe any pain.
"That 'hat' is a big band-aid Abe needs to keep on his
head. How about you just give Abe a gentle smooch,
Jermaine." She walked to Abe's left side and they both
kissed him. Then Jermaine hopped into a wheelchair
and started maneuvering it.

Monica sat on the edge of the bed and sighed. "Niko tried to prepare me for how you looked, but I didn't picture you so ...broken—you know—with the turban thing and the chest bandaging. Well, I'll just consider you my birthday present, all wrapped up!"

Abe sipped ice water from a straw, then asked, "Your birthday?"

"Yup! Next Thursday." She added, "Don't sound so excited."

"Sorry." Abe then read his card. A "Get Well" rhyme was followed by:

> I'm sorry we argued in the library. I'm not trying to be nosy, but you can be open with me. I'm a big girl. I can handle anything. Please don't shut me out.
> I love you. Monica

Wow, love, Abe thought. Maybe she could handle love, but he doubted himself. "Thank you," he said to her expectant face. He couldn't say those three words now, or even soon; his mind was too full of hateful images. Crunching his ice, he wondered how much Monica knew about the accident. Vanessa's story, that the car door had opened on a curve and Abe was thrown out, must have made it around school by now. Abe decided he wasn't going to offer Monica any extra information unless she saw through the lie. Even though she'd pledged to stick with him, the truth was just too awful.

Monica cleared her voice and said, "In case you want to catch up with school work, I brought some books and a few assignments."

"I'm supposed to say, 'thanks?'"

"Yes!" She added with sarcasm. "I was positive that you'd rather study physics than watch sports and cute nurses all day long." She stacked Abe's books on the floor.

"Can I do anything for you?" Monica asked. "How 'bout a foot massage?"

"Cool," Abe said, brightening.

While rubbing Abe's feet, Monica gave a rundown of school happenings since the accident: Leisha set a basketball team record for three-pointers, Justin's appointment for the Naval Academy came through, and she herself got an A+ on her Shakespeare term paper. She finished with, "I told Coach I was going to visit you. He said, 'hi, hurry back.'"

"Who's running my leg of the relay?" Abe asked gloomily, realizing he'd let the team down, again.

"I don't know," Monica said. "They tried out these two freshman at practice today. We'll find out at the meet tomorrow."

Without an ounce of sympathy, Abe pictured Khalid. He'd probably finish first three meets in a row. Khalid certainly wouldn't miss Abe.

"Hey, we got our social studies exams back yesterday. I got a 98. Here's your test, a 74. Abe, what happened? We'd just studied that stuff in the library."

"I don't know. I couldn't concentrate."

Abe watched her intense face, half-listening to her summary of the National Honor Society meeting. How would she have taken the news of Abe's suicide? Would she have felt worthless, or guilty? That would have been wrong, painful. But would she think he was subhuman if she knew the truth?

On Saturday, Abe moved to a private room, but in the *juvenile* psychiatric ward. After all, he wasn't eighteen yet. He didn't mind it until all the patients had been gathered in small groups: "Walky Talky" for kids ten and under; and "Teen Scene" for kids eleven to eighteen. Nobody was close to his age. He felt like Gulliver, in a wheelchair.

After introductions, the psychologist, Miss Jean, asked, "Before I suggest a topic, does anyone have something on their minds?"

Well, that was a stupid question. The patients wouldn't have been here if they didn't have anything on their minds.

Richie, probably the youngest in the group, shot his hand in the air. "Everybody is stealing my *Star Wars* action figures!"

"Not all of them—I only borrowed Princess Leah," replied Tess.

"Now children, you know that no one is allowed to have small toys in their rooms," said Miss Jean, not much older than Abe himself. "They're choking hazards."

She redirected her gaze at Richie and said, "Remember, this is a friendly place, Richie. Everyone likes you, and nobody wants to make you sad. I know you get nervous when you can't find belongings. But try not to think that the worst possible thing is always happening to you. Can anyone tell me how Richie can handle this situation in the future?"

A young teenage girl said, "He should check up his butt."

Abe suppressed a smile.

"Be nice," said Miss Jean.

Tess said, "Rich should nicely ask people instead of

accusing everybody right away. And he should share more."

"That's right," said the Doctor. "Tess, you get a star today. Two more stars and you get an extra half hour at bedtime."

"Someone stole my stars," Richie hollered. "I had enough, and now I don't!"

Abe rolled his eyes, then rolled right out of the room.

"Yoohoo! Abraham! Come back!" the doctor called after him.

He heard an announcement for assistance, and wondered if it was for him. He needed assistance, but not that idiotic jabbering. Before he even reached his room, two huge guys in green scrubs caught up with him.

"Whoa, whoa, whoa, buddy! Where you going so fast?" intoned a man who stepped in front of him. He gripped the handles of Abe's chair, giving Abe an eyeful of bulging biceps and triceps. Abe had never seen muscles so big on a white guy—well maybe old footage of Schwarzenegger.

The aide in back hit the wheelchair brakes.

Abe didn't have the strength to struggle. "Listen, I don't belong here."

"That's what all the patients say," said Mr. Body Builder.

Abe almost smiled. "What I mean is I might belong in a psych ward, but with the adults, not the seven-year-olds who still pee in their pants."

"Plenty of adults pee in their pants too."

Abe actually liked this guy. Hopefully, he worked the whole floor. "My dad is Dr. Elders in the ER here. Let me call him please, and he can get me transferred."

The aides wheeled Abe to the nurse's station and got him a phone. Abe left a message on George's voicemail.

"Can I just wait here until he calls back?" Abe asked a nurse.

"Sorry, no. You need to be supervised, and there's no one free here."

"So it's back to 'Teen Scene' for you!"

Abe groaned. When the big aide dropped him back to group therapy, Abe asked, "What's your name?"

"Woodrow. But people call me Woody." He picked up Abe's left arm and read the hospital bracelet. "Abraham—another presidential name! That's cool."

Later, on the adult floor, Abe felt better. Here, the patients were either sedated into a stupor, or doing sad, irrational things like trying to diaper a baby doll. Some simply wandered the halls. Their patches of hair stuck up like antennae. Abe wondered what tormenting wars waged inside of them.

Four o'clock, Abe's family would meet in his room. Abe wanted everything off his chest. He wanted Vanessa, George and Niko to know how horrible he really was. If they were going to un-adopt him, and deport him, let it be done quickly. He didn't want to be responsible for any more pain.

Dr. Carlson met briefly with Abe beforehand. "You really want me to tell them everything?"

Abe nodded. "I don't want any secrets. They can't decide what to do with me if they don't know everything."

"But you're still learning about your past, too."

"Well, we'll take it as it comes."

"All right," Dr. Carlson said. "For now, I'll talk in general about your past, and if you want to fill in any details, go right ahead."

Abe took a deep breath—which raked his chest—and said, "Let's go."

Niko bounded in first and clasped Abe's hand. "Yo! look at you. You're almost as handsome as I am."

Abe forced a grin, and raised his bed to a sitting position.

"Niko's right," Vanessa said, kissing Abe's cheek. "The swelling in your face has gone down a lot."

"Hey, Son," George said, subdued. He sat next to Niko, while Vanessa stood behind them both.

Dr. Carlson summed up the horrific events Abe had suffered. While they winced now and then, George and Niko took it in calmly. But Vanessa clutched their shoulders as if she were trying to stay above water. Next the Doctor brought up "James" and discussed dissociation.

"Isn't that's like multiple personality disorder?" Vanessa asked.

"You mean Jekyll & Hyde?" Niko wanted to know.

"If Abe had assumed a number of personalities over a long period of time, that might be his diagnosis," Dr. Carlson said. "But Abe only used his dissociated self, James, at the most extremely dangerous times."

"Such as?" George asked.

"Such as the heat of battle," Dr. Carlson replied. He shot a glance at Abe, who pointed back at him. "And during abuse."

Abe didn't elaborate with details. He actually felt detached, hearing these facts repeated by his psychiatrist. The words didn't hurt as much. His eyes met his doctor's compassionate, yet serious ones. Abe gulped, wondering how the next news was going to sound. Less barbaric? How would his family take it, that their adopted son, their frog-turned-prince, was a murderer?

"In order to accept this next revelation, to process it and deal with it," Dr. Carlson told Abe's family, "you must understand something very important. Abe and other kids—eight, nine, twelve-years old—were enslaved. They were routinely drugged and threatened. If they didn't do what their captors ordered, the boys might have a limb hacked off, or have a family member killed in front of them."

Abe spoke up. "One officer liked to have the boys kill their own families."

Vanessa whimpered.

"So the boys would become as guilty, as monstrous, as the adult soldiers themselves," Dr. Carlson stated. "These so-called adults trained them to kill, made them clear mine fields, become suicide bombers, pushed them into battle. They also sexually abused many of them."

Niko looked like he was going to puke.

George bit his lips, and shook his head. "I should have known," he murmured. "I did know, but not Abe, not Abe." George cleared his throat, but his voice still shook. "Is this what happened to you, Son?"

Abe's teeth were chattering. It sent spears of hot pain up his fractured face. He managed to nod.

"Yes," Dr. Carlson agreed, "but listen! Abe, the loving son and brother you cherish, only survived by creating that alter ego. *James* was the one who became the soldier. *James* was the one who was abused. The dissociation was a coping method."

Finally getting it, Niko jumped and blurted, "Wait! James is, was, Abe?"

"Yes," Abe whispered.

"That all happened to *you*?"

"Yes," Abe whispered. The word felt like glass in his throat.

"Yes, and no, Niko," Dr. Carlson corrected. "Bodily, physically, it happened. But mentally, Abe separated himself to stay safe and whole."

Silence consumed them, like the silence that holds soldiers hostage before launching an ambush. Niko slid down the wall to crouch in the corner. Was it the self-preservation instinct, Abe wondered, like if I can't see him, I can't kill him?

Vanessa's question was so quiet, Dr. Carlson asked her to repeat it.

Vanessa tilted her head as if it were too heavy to hold straight. "Did Abe, I mean James, kill...more than once? More than one person?"

Dr. Carlson glanced at Abe for an answer. Abe stared into Vanessa's eyes and said, "Yes."

Vanessa gasped and she withdrew to the window. George followed to console her. His eyes wide as bread plates, Niko crawled back into his chair. "Oh man, oh man, oh man," he kept saying.

Abe felt disgusting and disgusted. All alone again. Nobody reached out to *him*. No one consoled *him*. No one wanted to be near him. He didn't deserve them anyway.

Just then, Dr. Carlson said, "Abe, the worst is over. We only go up from here."

"Yeah, right," Abe whispered, watching George lead Vanessa into the hall.

"Abe, you okay?" Dr. Carlson asked. "You don't seem agitated."

"Yeah I'm all right, except I gotta take a leak."

"Okay, I'll run after your parents, and we'll be right

back. Niko, please stay with Abe for a few minutes. He shouldn't be left alone."

Standing at the toilet, Abe realized that this was his first piss since his catheters were removed that afternoon. The tip of his dick was a little tender, but it felt liberating to see those old bubbles again. He chided himself. How could he be thinking about something so stupid while his parents were dealing with news of their murderous adopted son? Well, they should be thankful he wasn't their son by blood. It's not like they conceived him and their genes sucked.

Abe shuffled toward the window, gazing out. "Whoa—ow!" he exclaimed, almost tripping over Niko's legs. Abe sat down next to him. Niko scooted his chair away a foot.

Without looking at Abe, Niko asked, "Who are you right now? Abe or James? Should I be afraid—shit, I'm already afraid of you!"

"Don't be, Niko. I'm better—I don't know if I'm *all* better. But living with you, and with George and Vanessa, has been the best thing in my life." Abe started to say that he'd never hurt the family. But he had. Actually and already, he had. He went to pat Niko's shoulder, but Niko leaned out of reach. When Abe returned to bed, Niko bolted to the bathroom. Abe heard water running, but it didn't cover Niko's sounds of retching.

About ten minutes later, Dr. Carlson brought George and Vanessa back. They had coffee in their hands and a soda for Niko, who took it like a crackhead grabs a vial. After a long gulp, he stared down at it instead of meetings Abe's eyes.

George actually looked worse than Vanessa. He began, "Abe, Dr. Carlson has told us the *good* news that you won't be held accountable for, for, for your actions in Liberia. There are agencies working for clemency for the child soldiers."

Abe wanted Vanessa's reaction. She'd been quiet, too quiet, and staying in the background. Abe asked her, "How do *you* feel about what I did?"

"You were a child," Vanessa said. "It wasn't your fault, but still...."

Abe caught that bit of doubt at the end and dreaded what she would say next.

George jumped in. "Abe, we adopted you four years ago, knowing you'd been traumatized. We took on the responsibility of raising you. It's like a marriage— through good times and bad, in sickness and in health."

"Yeah," Niko spoke under his breath, "this is some fucked-up sickness."

Dr. Carlson pressed his hands down to quiet the discussion. "Four years ago, we dealt with Abe's grief, adoption, and assimilation issues. Now we have, pardon the pun, new hurdles to clear. The question is: how do we handle this new aspect of Abe's PTSD, his post traumatic stress?"

"Wwww wait—what do you call it?" Niko interrupted.

"His flashbacks, nightmares, confusing behavior," George explained.

"Oh."

Dr. Carlson clapped once and said, "I want to try a technique that goes beyond bringing out the memories, to actually *treat* the traumatic emotions. It's called EMDR."

"What's with all these initials?" Niko asked.

"Don't worry," Dr. Carlson said. "EMDR has done wonders with war veterans. And I will include facets

of other successful treatments such as cognitive behavioral therapy."

"You're losing me worser, man," Niko said.

Dr. Carlson said, "Calm down, Niko. You don't need
to spit this back out on a test. I'll give you some literature to read at home."

George asked, "What about other treatments—group
therapy, coping skills?"

Dr. Carlson replied, "I run a great PTSD support
group every Thursday evening. Abe will learn more
coping skills and can let out his experiences and feelings with people who have 'been there.' And this time,
I'm demanding a long commitment." George and Abe
locked eyes. Over the past few years, George had always been pestering Abe to go to group more often.
Now Abe mouthed, "I know. I know."

"Well, that's down the road anyway. I'd like to start
EMDR and therapy here immediately, while Abe is a
patient."

"Here?" Abe interjected. "I have to stay here? How
long?"

"For as long as it takes—hopefully, no longer than
two weeks to get you through the worst of your past.
Then I can see you as an outpatient again."

George stepped forward and agreed. "It's the safest
thing to do, Abe. And think, I'll probably see you more
here than I would have at home."

"Are there any more questions?" Dr. Carlson asked.
After a brief silence,

he said, "Vanessa, you seem awfully quiet. Do you
have any specific concerns?"

Vanessa debated herself for a few seconds, then began haltingly. "I have to admit—sorry, Abe, but this is
the truth—that I'm afraid. ...I'm afraid for Niko's life,

my husband's, my own, and what about his school community? I hate feeling like this—I should know better—I have psychology training! But when the violence, the depravity, hits home...this isn't easy to take!"

"What I wanna know is," Niko challenged, "can you honestly tell us that this 'James' dude will never come back?"

"Yeah," Abe spoke up. "Can you promise that?"

Dr. Carlson's eyes closed. That was enough of a 'no' that Vanessa buried her face in George's chest. He held her shaking body. Niko added his arms around Vanessa forming a tight impenetrable trio.

Fighting his own tears, Abe didn't know where to look. So that was it. He was no longer a part of this family, this beautiful, talented family who had saved his life. Almost.

CHAPTER FOURTEEN

Out of the twenty beds on this wing, Abe counted only
a few patients who were noticeably mentally ill. Many
just looked bored or sour. He kept his eye on two in
particular. A forty-year-old man, Gus, had fallen in
love with the fire extinguisher inside its case. Every
time he passed it, he would caress it and say, "I know
what it's like to be kept in a cage." He was blind as
a mole and could talk a water fountain off the wall.
Besides the blindness, what did Gus have wrong with
him? He looked fine. Damien, the angry guy with the
hair all stuck up, was goth or punk, only dressed in
hospital whites instead of black. He was always arguing about the stupid rules. Like no jewelry. "My fucking seventeen holes will close up! The hospital better pay for every goddam re-piercing!" Damien, who
smelled of cigarettes, also had walking pneumonia.
He enjoyed making the sucking noises of post-nasal
drip. Then he'd swallow the phlegm with gusto.

On Monday, Abe began group therapy. At least it
didn't have a stupid name. He had to go twice a day,
at 10 am and again at 4 pm. A female resident named

Dr. Yang wheeled him and his IV stand into a big sunny room. She introduced him, and the crowd of ten chimed, "Hi, Abe."

Yang positioned him right next to her and asked, "Abe, why don't you tell us about yourself?"

Abe took a deep breath. It hurt to breathe. It hurt to speak. Plus, he didn't feel like spilling his guts to people he didn't even know. Then again, he didn't know Dr. Carlson at first, either.

"Well, I'm from Liberia," Abe began. That info met a lot of blank expressions. He added, "That's on the west coast of Africa."

"Africa! That's far away," said Gert, somebody's grandmother with a brace around her neck.

Gus spoke up. "My sight isn't so good, but I thought you looked mighty dark."

Yang scolded, "Now, Gus, no comments about race."

"I didn't mean—"

"That's okay, Gus," Abe said. "There are people of all colors in Africa."

"I know!" Gus replied. "I go on safari there all the time, and the white people are the ones you give your money to."

A lot of patients nodded. They had vivid imaginations.

Yang said, "Now everybody, it's not time for your stories. Abe is telling his."

Abe wondered how much of anyone's stories Dr. Yang believed.

"So why did you leave Africa?" Gus asked. "Too hot?"

"No. A doctor brought me here to escape a war. My family was killed and I had nobody left. So now I live with his family in Maryland."

"Maryland! That's far away," said Gert.

"Is your new family dark like you?" Gus wanted to know.

Damien, the goth, said, "Gus, is your family stupid like you?"

Abe nodded a thanks to Damien.

Yang asked, "Abe, do you want to tell us why you're here?"

Abe shrugged. He looked around and wondered if the other patients had tried to kill themselves too? He bet none of them tried to kill others. Nobody here would understand what he'd gone through. "When I was young, I was captured by rebels. They forced me to be a soldier. And I killed people. And now I'm trying to deal with it."

"Cool," said Damien, massaging the six empty holes on his ear.

Gert paled and scooted her wheelchair farther back from Abe.

Gus piped up, "I killed people before, too, but not in Africa!"

Abe glanced at Yang to see if he believed Gus's story. She gave him a curt nod, then quickly resumed her professional role.

Abe prayed that Gus would keep far away from him. He shivered to consider the ways in which Gus may have killed people. With his bad eyesight, it must have been close up. But the guy was so damn friendly. Maybe that's how he lured his victims.

Yang addressed the group, "Many of us are here because we're trying to deal with problems such as death. Would anyone else like to talk about dying?"

Eight of the ten raised their hands. Gert didn't. She just said, "Death! That's far away."

Abe groaned inside. He admitted, he was sick, but not half as warped as these people.

That night, Monica was coming over. Abe checked himself in the bathroom mirror. He looked as bad as he felt, and he felt like crap. The Percoset didn't work on his headache; it only made him sleepy. He couldn't get over the mummy bandaging on his head. Worse, his hair was growing all itchy under the wrap, and he was dying to shave it all off like before. The last time he had hair was the last time he'd seen Grant four years ago. Many of the rebels went bald—that way, the lice couldn't latch on.

Abe had warned Monica on the phone about visiting restrictions. Dr. Carlson almost didn't approve of her visit, since sexual situations could trigger a flashback. But George had convinced him to let her come.

"What could we possibly get away with?" Abe had asked him. "A supervising nurse will be there."

Dr. Carlson gave Abe a sly look, and said, "Okay, no touching at all. Not even a kiss hello."

"You're cold, man!" Abe moaned.

Soft puffy furniture filled the visitors' room—no metal in sight. Far overhead, over-bright fluorescent lights beamed down. No way to reach the pulsating bars of glass, even if you stood on the couch. One wall was wired glass, separating the supervisor from the room. Abe came in through that booth. Monica had just come through, too—both of them frisked and metal-detected clean. Speakers from the room into the booth would make their conversation anything but private. A camera in an upper corner recorded every move, every word.

"Hey," Monica said, keeping her distance. "Still got that thing?" She pointed to his IV.

"Yeah, it sucks," Abe said. "But it will be gone starting tomorrow, when I can start on liquids. I can't eat solid food for a few more days."

"Well, you let me know when you can, and I'll cook up something good."

"Like ribs? I'd do anything for some scorching ribs."

"Anything you want." Monica sat at the opposite end of the couch and rummaged in her backpack. "I got more of your assignments."

Abe reached to take the textbooks, but they were too heavy and fell. "I got no strength on my right side, Monica," he admitted while she picked up the books. "I really messed myself up. I'm not even sure about track this spring."

Monica placed the books on an empty seat and said, "Shhh, one thing at a time, Abe. Just you get well, totally healed up, and then you can worry about track. Track's not going anywhere, you know what I mean?"

"Yeah, but my scholarships—"

Monica changed the subject. "Madame Clairmont said you can do this French test as a take-home. She said she'd pray for you."

Abe glanced over the test: irregular verb conjugations in three different tenses. He could use the prayers! At least he had all the time in the world to study.

"Check this out. Blalock's being all nice with me. I think she wants to kiss and make-up with us."

"The thought of kissing her makes me wanna puke."

"No kissing, no physical contact at all," came a stern voice from the booth.

Monica sighed.

Abe had heard and seen that sigh before.

Frustration laced it. How many times had he backed off from her? She probably thought he got hurt on purpose. Well, Abe recalled, didn't I?

Suddenly Monica blurted, "All this security kind of freaks me out. It's like a prison in here. How come?"

"Carlson worries that I might hurt myself or shut down. Have another one of those spells. Here, I get therapy twenty-four seven, so I get better faster."

"Oh, okay," Monica said quietly. She peered through the wired glass to see down the corridor. "Are there any dangerous people here?"

Abe almost laughed. "Yeah," he answered honestly.

"Murderers?"

"Yeah." She was breathing the same air with one right now.

Monica fished through her backpack and came out with her tape recorder. "Can I interview one for our school newspaper?"

Abe huffed. She wanted to tell the world about all us locked-up sickos.

"What?" Monica asked. "I know I might need the Doctor's permission and a guard and all that. And of course I won't use their real names. Hey, I'm going to ask that nurse over there how I can set it up."

"Don't, Mon—"

And off she sped to the door and pressed the buzzer. A minute later, she returned with the name and number of the hospital public affairs officer. She flipped open her Blackberry and checked her availability. Abe couldn't take his eyes off her.

"Why are you staring at me?"

"What could you possibly want to know about crazy criminals?" Abe asked.

Her eyes wide, she squealed, "I've got a million

questions! Let me try some out on you." Abe shook his head, but Monica held an air-microphone to her mouth and asked, "Do you understand what you did? Are you capable of feeling sorry? When you were my age, did you have powerful urges to hurt people?"

Abe felt dread close his throat. He could answer every one of them. His nerves pulsed. He felt thirteen again, a dangerous instinct he couldn't control. Fight or flight. Every inch of his body tightened. He needed for Monica to leave. Right now! Remove her. Remove her! He couldn't. He wasn't in control. Remove himself. He sprang up, grimacing. He lurched for the buzzer and banged on the door.

"Let me out! Now!" he screamed.

"Abe? What's going on?" Monica asked.

"Nurse, let me out!"

"Did I do something? Say something? Whatever, I'm sorry."

The nurse fumbled with the paging system then shouted an order.

"Talk to me, Abe!" Monica cried out. "I don't understand."

"Nobody does!" Abe grunted.

"But I want to! Please don't go. I'm sorry!"

A moment later Woody appeared in the booth. The door buzzed open and Abe fell into his arms.

"You okay, my man?" Woody asked.

"I need some air," Abe heaved.

Woody walked Abe down the hall. Monica repeated his name, pleading for an answer. Just the other night, Abe couldn't imagine life without Monica. Now, he couldn't take her being so close to the disgusting truth. Then she'd hate him and spread his bloody story across Page 1.

He had to cut her loose. He glanced behind and saw her crying. Her palms pressed flat against the wall, Monica was now safe from him. He'd make sure she stayed that way.

CHAPTER FIFTEEN

The next morning, Abe left at least six messages on Niko's voice mail. After school, Niko finally called back. His voice was clipped.

"I only got two minutes til practice, so make it quick," he stated.

Abe felt like he was talking to a stranger. "Just tell Coach you were checking in on me," Abe explained. "He'll—"

"Yo, I gotta go."

"Wait!" Abe blurted his request.

"Don't dump your shit on me," Niko said. "No way *I'm* telling Monica you're bouncing."

"Come on, Niko, all you have to say is 'Abe feels he's too fucked up now and doesn't want to drag you down.'"

"Yeah right, Abe. Then, knowing her, she'll say, 'He's not dragging me down. I want to help lift him up.' That's the way she is. She won't take 'no' from me. She's gonna be in your face big time."

"Tell her even *you're* scared of me."

Niko didn't respond, probably 'cause it was true.

An idea popped into Abe's head. "Hey, I can have her banned from the ward. They won't let her in."

Niko forced a laugh. Did he want himself banned?

Abe persisted. "So, tell her tomorrow after track practice, okay?"

"I'll try," Niko muttered. "Gotta go."

Abe felt weird going into Dr. Carlson's office at the hospital. Instead of his warm kitchen smelling of good food, his office smelled sterile and dusty at the same time. Instead of a guy's hang-out with a pool table, his shelves were piled high with books. His desk looked orderly: a small pile of papers on his right; a phone and intercom machine in the center; and to his left a picture of his wife. The frame read: *You Drive Me Crazy.*

Woody transported Abe in a wheelchair, and positioned him in the center of the room. "I'll park my ass right outside the door," he said.

"Sheeet," Abe said, "Then I guess I gotta jump from the window."

After hello's, Dr. Carlson moved Abe into a corner, grabbed a chair for himself, and drew a white screen around them. On a small stand were a metronome, a tape recorder, and a glass of water. Even the ceiling was a boring white. No cobwebs. No pulsating bars of fluorescent light.

"So tell me how this new thing—this bunch of initials—is better or different than hypnosis," Abe wanted to know.

"There are several differences," Dr. Carlson noted, "but mainly, with EMDR, you're fully awake and alert."

Abe liked that.

"Basically," Dr. Carlson continued, "scientists think that the original trauma shuts down the left part of the brain that processes grief. EMDR helps open and energize that half, so the patient can *fully* deal with the problem and get over it."

"Sounds too good to be true," Abe said.

"Plus it improves the patient quickly. Note, I didn't say 'cures,' but EMDR sort of opens the door for other therapies to work."

"Okay, let's do it," Abe said.

Dr. Carlson directed, "Follow the back and forth motion of this metronome. It will help the left side of your brain process these memories. Kind of like how a good car can jump-start a weak car."

Abe's brow wrinkled. "I've never jump-started a car."

Dr. Carlson put his hands on his hips. "Okay, wise guy, you know what I mean. Now, tell me about that day your mother and sister tried to escape. Start at the beginning and relate any detail that comes into your mind—even tying your shoes—in the order it happened."

"Man, I told you that story ten times already."

"Well, only twice, but repeating the traumatic memory forces you to dig deeper into it, to look for different details. The act of repeating the event makes it mundane—boring actually, and no longer powerful over you."

Abe let out a big puff of air. "Okay, if you say so."

Dr. Carlson pressed the record button and started the metronome.

Abe watched it for a few moments, picked up on its monotonous beat, and started talking: "You said you want details. Well, I never had to tie my shoes when I got up. That's because I never took them off—they'd be stolen in a second. I even wore them when we bathed in a stream or lake. They were filthy and smelly, but not too many kids had shoes at all. Every raid, there'd be more shoes, more food, more guns. One time—"

"Abe, let's stick to that one day. You stood up and then...."

"I smelled coffee. I started to like the taste of it, too. I had to wake up the boys, about forty of us, scattered in lean-to's, and lead them inside the factory. We had to help deliver breakfast to the troops. There were so many of them, now that the Khran had joined us. I don't know why—Gio and Khran didn't usually get along.

"When I went inside the factory, I always tried to see my mother and Ellie. Even though they didn't care about me anymore. That morning, my mother was spooning dumboy into buckets. Ellie was washing potatoes. The ears of that stupid pink bunny were flopping out of her skirt pocket. I don't know why—but I used to hate that thing. At home, I was always hiding it from her. Seeing Mom and Ellie working hard eased my mind a bit. As long as they could work, the rebels would keep them alive."

"You mentioned 'dumboy?' I never heard of that. What is it?"

"Mashed cassava. We usually had potatoes and onions around too. I'd just set the food down and run off. The rebels were like hyenas on an antelope. I was afraid they'd eat me, too. I'd heard stories about that! I know it doesn't sound like such a bad chore, but delivering the food was torture! We were starving! But

Grant told us, 'You filch any of that food before the soldiers eat, I'm going to sew your mouths up.' And I already knew all about Grant's sewing talent.

"After breakfast, we didn't do any raiding. Grant sent out scouts, to see where we should go next. We were waiting on 'intelligence,' Grant called it. So we did drills all day, mostly hand-to-hand combat. The officers showed us kids where to kick and bite and slash with our knives. We practiced with each other first, but then Grant made us practice with the grown men because we'd be coming across them in combat.

"'Punch those balls, kids! Slash them behind their knees, behind their ankles. Use your short size as an advantage!'"

"Wait, Abe. Don't jump to the evening." Dr. Carlson paused the metronome. "How did that sparring make you feel?"

"I felt confident and strong when I was practicing with kids my age. But I didn't want to go against a big man—even if it was just practice."

"Just because he was bigger?"

"No...I was afraid he might have seen me before, with Grant or someone else, you know, doing that nasty stuff. I was scared *he* might try something nasty."

"Okay, let's continue." Dr. Carlson restarted the metronome.

"We gave out lunch—bread, and fish some guys caught in the river that used to power the factory. For once, there was plenty of leftover food, so us kids ate and ate until our stomachs burst. After lunch, it started raining. We tried to sleep inside our lean-to's, because you never knew when you might have time to sleep again. I was dozing but shouts woke me up. A Gio and a Khran had gotten into an argument over who could sleep inside an abandoned car in the factory parking lot. They started punching, and everybody crowded around them, yelling, 'Fight, fight, fight, fight.'

"I thought, don't these men know how to do anything else? I didn't want to watch, but then I heard Grant's voice. Grant and a Khran officer, now in the middle of the crowd, each held his man by his hair. Grant said, 'We fight together. We do not fight each other. The next time I see such a crime, this will happen to you.'

"I couldn't believe it! Grant slid his knife across the neck of the Gio rebel, a brother. Then the Khran officer killed his man, too. I covered my eyes, a split second before blood spurt against my hands....
Dr. Carlson, I didn't remember that before. Maybe it didn't really happen."

Dr. Carlson paused the metronome and said, "What was in your mind then? How did you get the blood off?"

Abe listened for the metronome clicks again. They felt soothing, almost, like the sound of a drummer tapping his rim. "I felt dirty. I found a puddle and used mud to wash the blood off. Then I tried to go back to sleep. But my hands itched, and my stomach felt queasy. I'd never seen Grant do something like that. Others? Yeah. But I thought Grant was better than them, more like high class. It scared me, thinking about how easy he did it."

Dr. Carlson commented, "That would scare anybody."

"We served dinner like usual. The men had fish and yams. We ate local rice, that's all that night. After, we passed the flattened cardboard. I needed to find my mother and Ellie. I hated that they were mad at me. I wanted to make them understand I was following orders just to stay alive.

"On the way, I saw them creeping along the outside wall. I whispered, 'Mom! What are you doing?'

"'Son,' she said, 'I know this area well. I have an old friend here. We're going to her house. Come with us!'

"'You better not turn us in, Abe,' Ellie made Bunny say.

Abe shook his head. "'But the rebels will kill us if they catch us!' I said. 'They're monsters.'

"'The rebels are killing us day in and day out,' my mother explained, locking eyes with me.

"She was right. The work and the punishments and the constant yelling. On top of that, their hatred grew on us like mold. I told my mother I'd help. I got her friend's address, and maybe I could join them. Before I left, Ellie actually said, 'Please come.'

"I distracted a guard for ten minutes. Then I heard shots and I heard screaming—a girl kind. I saw Mom and Ellie taken back into the factory. I followed the hollering to a corner room all lit up. But the windows were too high, I couldn't climb anything or see anything. There were shots, again. I didn't hear screaming any more...."

Abe hunched over and said, "I think I'm all done for now, Dr. Carlson."

"You don't remember anything more about that night? Did you tell anybody what you saw? Did you go to sleep?"

Abe shook his head.

"Okay," Dr. Carlson said, turning off the metronome. "Abe, it must have been devastating to hear your mother and sister in pain."

Abe stifled a sob and said, "I didn't do anything to help them."

Dr. Carlson leaned over and held Abe's hands. "What could you have done? You couldn't see in. If you'd barged through the door—which was probably guarded—you would have been shot on the spot."

"I wish I was shot, shot dead. At least, we'd all be in heaven together."

"Easy, Abe," Dr. Carlson said. "I understand how life might seem so hopeless right now. But you still have so much worthwhile living to do. If you couldn't help your mother, you can still help other people."

Abe wiped his sleeve across his face and sat up straight. Dr. Carlson handed him the tissue box.

After a moment, Abe said, "I can't believe I forgot all about that fight."

"I don't blame you," Dr. Carlson said. "It was too horrible a memory to walk around with."

"Now that I think about it, Grant was a monster, two-faced. If you got him mad, look out. He'd slaughter anybody in his way. And the more people watching, the more he liked it."

"Yes, perhaps. Lots of people like to show off."

"Not me."

"Oh no? Don't you want to perform well when your girlfriend is around?"

Abe pictured breaking the tape at the end of the race, with Monica cheering beyond the finish line. "Okay, Doc. Yeah, I gotcha."

Dr. Carlson continued, "Seriously, I think 'James' thrived on attention like Grant did. Whereas you, Abe, didn't want any part of what James did."

Abe mumbled, "I wish I could believe that."

Dr. Carlson removed the screen and suddenly the

room opened up to Abe. Colors and shapes flowed into his eyes. He had thought the office was sterile. But now he could see two still life paintings on the wall opposite the book case, a spider plant in the corner with baby plants springing out on their own spider silks. A small stained glass panel in the window cast green, gold and red light on the beige carpeting. Everything was still very neat, but it looked warmer, more like Dr. Carlson's home.

Maybe this wouldn't be so bad after all.

CHAPTER SIXTEEN

Abe felt wiped out the rest of Tuesday. He slept on and off, between the pokings and proddings of nurses. At one point, he heard a nurse say, "Gus, that's awfully nice of you to share your dessert with Abe, but he's sleeping now. Besides he can't have solid food yet."

"Oh," Gus said. "Would you like to share my Jell-O?"

The nurse laughed and said, "No, but thank you, Gus. You're such a gentleman."

Gus's voice faded as the conversation moved down the hall.

During the night, Abe had smelled George's after shave. Abe dreamed of sleeping at home, across the room from Niko. After his shift, George always came in, kissed them, and tucked them in like five-year-olds.

The next morning, Woody came in early—6 am. "Come on, Abe, let's get up and get washed. Your internist will be here in fifteen minutes."

Abe had almost forgotten about his physical injuries. They were nothing compared to his mental pain.

And he didn't know what was giving him headaches—his concussion or his memories?

"I can do it myself," he said, as Woody started into the bathroom after him.

"Deal?" Woody said. "Go ahead and do your best, but I'll bathe from the chest up, since you're all bandaged."

"Deal," Abe said.

A doctor Abe had only seen once before strode in the room. Without saying hello, he checked all the fresh vitals on the chart, while Woody helped Abe take his johnny off. "If you pass inspection today, young man," said the doctor, "you can move up to a liquid diet as we'd planned."

"Finally, something to taste," Abe said.

"Huh! That's a good one," Woody quipped.

The doctor felt just about everything with and without his stethoscope. Abe thought the doctor should have a "breathe, don't breathe" signal on him like the "walk, don't walk" ones. Breathing deeply still hurt, but Abe had less tenderness where his diaphragm had been punctured.

Next, the doctor examined Abe's head and then his reflexes. Abe walked a straight line, stood on one foot, touched his nose. It was beginning to feel like one of Ellie's stupid games. Ellie.... He'd do anything to play a stupid game with her now.

"You're healing quite nicely," the doctor said. "I'm approving your move to bland liquid diet including dairy. We can disconnect the IV, but we'll be leaving the port in your arm. Have a nice day." He turned on his heel and vanished.

"Nice bedside manner, don't you think?" said Woody.

Abe grinned.

"I'll be up with breakfast in a few minutes. Do you like coffee or tea?"

"Coffee, please."

Abe wondered, what exactly *is* a liquid diet? He pictured a refrigerator case in a store. He doubted they'd let him have root beer, his favorite. What about the sports drinks? Probably too much sugar.

Woody returned with a loaded tray: coffee, a fruit and yogurt smoothie, and Jell-O.

"Not bad," Abe said.

"The smoothies, at least, are decent," Woody said. "I get them in the caf." He plopped some forms on the bed table and said, "I'll pick these up on my next round. Is there anything else I can get for you, your royal hiney-ness?"

Abe swallowed his coffee and said, "No, thanks."

Some forms were menus. What kind of bullion for lunch and dinner, and what flavor Jell-O. He'd be served V8 at each meal and drinkable yogurt.

Another form gave him his schedule for the day. In between group therapy sessions, physical therapy and meals, he'd have another session with Dr. Carlson. He wondered if George was on duty today or if Vanessa would stop by. She'd called a few times, but Abe hadn't seen her since Saturday. Tonight, Niko was supposed to come and report how everything went with Monica.

Group therapy was certainly lively. Dr. Yang asked, "Does anyone have a special topic to talk about today?" Damien took center stage. "I want my earrings and studs back, and so do Ellen, Leroy, and Rickie. I think the ban on metal goes too far. I mean, like I'm going to kill myself or somebody else with the stud of my diamond? Gimme a break!"

Gus said, "It would be very difficult to kill someone with a half-inch stud. You'd have to stun the victim first so it lies still, then place the stud exactly in the carotid artery and let the victim bleed out. Yes, very difficult to do. Now if—"

"Shut-up, Gus! You're a sicko," Damien said.

"That's enough," Dr. Yang said sternly.

Damien's eyes ranged around the room. "Abe, you with us?"

Abe shrugged. "I don't have anything pierced, but I'm down with you all."

Dr. Yang said, "Let's have a vote. If I can tell the administrators that this request has the approval of all the ambulatory pysch patients, they will look at the issue more seriously. But I can't guarantee anything. It may be more of a sanitary measure than a safety one."

The rest of the session passed by with Abe steeped in boredom. He kept thinking of Monica, how she took the break-up. He hoped she wasn't too hurt. She'd bounce back—she's got it together. She's got a lot to look forward to.

Hmm, that's what Dr. Carlson kept telling him. But Abe still had problems seeing into the next day.

George showed up at lunch and kissed Abe's forehead. "Look at this fancy spread!"

Abe smiled. "I'm dying to bite into something. Can't you smuggle in some pizza or chicken?"

"Doctor's orders," George reminded him, picking up his son's chart. "That would be a slap in your internist's face. Let me see, who is that? Oh! Mr. Congeniality!"

Abe laughed and his V8 went down the wrong pipe. He started coughing—God, that hurt! His whole chest felt like it was ripping apart.

"Man, I'm sorry," George said, coming to the bedside. "Calm down, Abe. There, little breaths at first."

Abe curled up, and George said, "No, keep your shoulders back. Open up your airways."

After a few minutes of steady breathing, Abe asked, "What's Vanessa doing these days, I mean, besides work?"

"She didn't visit yesterday?" George asked.

"I didn't see her. She might have tried to visit, but I could have been with Dr. Carlson or asleep."

"Hmm, maybe."

"George, she's freaked out about me, isn't she."

"Don't worry, we'll get through this," he said. He checked his watch and announced, "Break's over. I'll try to see you before I go home at three."

And they did see each other later, at Dr. Carlson's door. "Abe!" Dr. Carlson said, "It's good to see you walking down, instead of being wheeled."

"Yeah, they lifted some restrictions on me." He nodded at Woody, and added, "I still need my bodyguard."

"Well, not for long," George said. "According to Dr. Carlson here, you're doing well. That's great news, Abe. We'll have you home with us in no time."

Abe allowed another kiss from his father, who seemed to be in a very kissy mood lately. "Tomorrow—I come on at three. I'm going to talk with Vanessa, see exactly what's troubling her."

Dr. Carlson asked George, "Has she been to any of the family support group meetings?"

"I don't think so. I'll encourage it more strongly this time, even see if I can make one of the meetings."

"Good. She needs all the help she can get. And Niko?"

George looked at Abe for an answer. Abe shrugged

a shoulder. "He said he'd try to make it here after dinner."

"Great," said Dr. Carlson. "So, let's get to work."

As Abe was helping him with the screen and recorder, he asked, "How come I get to see you almost every day? I can't be your only patient."

"Want to know how many patients I have? 250! But not all of them are active, you know. Obviously, you are acutely active. Usually I see six to eight patients a day. Some of them are on your floor, but I'm not going to tell you who. Just like I don't discuss your case with anyone but colleagues who might help me with it."

Abe nodded. Fair enough.

After they got set up, Dr. Carlson asked Abe to recount his time at the factory, including the deaths of his mother and sister.

"Not again, Dr. Carlson. I'm getting sick of this stuff."

"Exactly! You're supposed to."

"Sheesh," Abe sighed.

Dr. Carlson told him what would be different this time. "Instead of you watching the metronome, you're going to close your eyes. I'm going to be tapping your right and left hands one at a time. Listen and feel for the taps, as you speak. I'll give you breaks like yesterday where we can dive deeper into your experience."

It sounded hokey, but Abe closed his eyes and let the hand-tapping begin. He launched into the morning and repeated his breakfast duties. Then came the hand-to-hand drills with the kids. "After that we had to practice with the men because we'd face them in fighting sometimes. I got this Khran guy who must have been a logger. He was tall and had huge muscles—he wasn't wearing a shirt, and he was shiny with sweat. And I told you, Gio and Khran never trusted each other. I tried to spar, but he put his hand on top of my head to keep me at arm's distance. He laughed the whole time and teased me, calling me 'a little girl, sweet boy'—that kind of stuff.

"An officer came by and told him, 'Cut it out. Let the kid get his moves in. He could save your life some time.'"

The tapping stopped on Abe's hands and he opened his eyes. Dr. Carlson asked, "When the Khran was doing that to you, what were you feeling?"

"I was embarrassed. Furious. I wanted to kill him, not spar with him."

"But he was so big."

"Yeah. After he stopped teasing me, I tried to spar, but he grabbed me and held me above his head, then dropped me in the mud. He'd be a great pro wrestler, the asshole."

"And nobody stopped him?"

"No. I felt pretty helpless. And I was mad, I mean, we were supposed to be on the same side. He did that three more times, and then I thought 'fuck him' and I ran off."

"Okay," said Dr. Carlson. "Close your eyes again and let's move on."

"I guess I slept, because I woke up when I heard guys fighting. Everybody was egging these two guys on, yelling, 'Fight, fight, fight, fight.' I wanted to see who was fighting, and it was that big Khran guy with one of our men. The Khran was winning, beating the shit out of our guy.

"Then I saw Grant separate the fighters, and Grant and a Khran captain grabbed their men by their hair.

Grant said, 'We fight together. We do not fight each other. The next time I see such a crime, this will happen to you.' He slit the Gio's throat! I couldn't believe it! Now, of course the Khran officer would have to kill his guy too. I clawed my way closer to see this. I smiled at the man who had teased me and threw me around like a rag doll. When the officer slit the man's throat, blood spurt out. Some hit my chin. It was hot, and I licked it off."

"Abe? Abe?" a man's voice called.

The hand taps stopped.

"Abe, are you there?"

Abe opened his eyes and exhaled forcefully. "Whoa.... I didn't remember all that. But now I can picture it so clearly. I felt like I had won, won a battle watching the big Khran die."

"Because that's what you wanted to happen, and it did happen, Abe. You didn't do it yourself...but did you enjoy watching it?"

Abe nodded. "Now I remember that Grant and I grinned a bit at each other. He told me he had seen what the big Khran was doing to me earlier. 'I didn't realize that I would get our revenge so soon, James,' Grant said. He gave me some pills to celebrate."

"How do you feel about Grant and the other officer's behavior now?"

"I don't think Grant should have killed our guy. Because he was getting beat up—that was enough punishment, embarrassment. And the big Khran started it, someone said."

"You know that for a fact?"

Abe hung his head and mumbled, "No."

"But it still pleased you to see him die."

"Yes, but...but now, it creeps me out."

"Yes...," Carlson said. He started the hand taps again. "Let's keep it going. Close your eyes and really focus on what comes into your mind next."

Abe recounted dinner and running into his mother and sister at the wall. "I forgot to tell you, I took the pills Grant gave me, because I was sort of nervous to go distract the guard. When I heard my mother and Ellie screaming. I followed the sound to a corner of the building all lit up. But the windows were too high. I didn't see any way to boost myself up either. I sneaked around, looking for a door. It was ajar! And there inside, I saw my mother and sister, face down, with soldiers on top of them. There were other men in a line, like that time they fucked Steven and me with the pails over our head. I couldn't let the same thing happen to my mother and sister!

"I burst in and picked up one of the guns leaning against a wall. There were shots. My shots! And I mowed down the men in line, just like they had taught me. I fired at the men on top of my mother and sister, and they rolled off, dead with their dicks sticking up in the air like flagpoles without flags. A door banged open and Grant and the Khran officer ran in.

"'Put your hands up,' I told them.

"'James, my boy,' said Grant.

"'I'm nobody's boy but my mother's and father's,' I yelled.

"'Please, give me the gun,' he said, all sing-songy. 'Come on, after all I've done for you?'

"'This is what you've done for me.' And I shot them both until they stopped twitching. I picked up two new guns and ran away."

The tapping stopped. "Open your eyes, Abe," said Dr. Carlson. "We need to talk about this."

Abe's lips trembled. He gazed at the ceiling as if it could nullify the horrors he'd just related. He bit down on his lips and peered at Dr. Carlson.

"Is that what happened, Abe, or what you'd *wanted* to happen?"

"You mean, is that true? I don't know! I don't know if I *want* it to be true."

"We'll go over it again tomorrow, a different way. Then we'll know for sure," said Dr. Carlson. "But we should treat it as the truth right now. Do you remember how you felt then? Was it the same as James and the convoy attack?"

Abe thought about going mad firing the gun after seeing Steven go down. "I think it was like that, yeah. Seeing my mother and sister made my whole body boil. Anger was yanking all my strings."

"Before you ran away, did you feel powerful?"

"A little, but mostly angry. Even when I stopped running, my veins were throbbing hot with it. I was wet with sweat, and shaking."

"Abe, were your mother and sister alive when you barged in?"

Abe frowned and cocked his head at the question. "Yes, they were screaming," he stated. "My back was to them at first, then I turned and shot at the men on top of them. I could barely see Ellie, she was so small. All I saw was that stupid bunny. She was clutching it, her arm sticking out from under a guy. I couldn't tell if they were alive, I don't know! They had just been screaming, they were alive, but they didn't get up. Oh God, oh God, did I kill them too? Don't tell me! I must have! I didn't shoot at Mom and Ellie, but at the men, but my mother and sister were so close. Oh God!"

Dr. Carlson threw his arms around Abe, but Abe

roared, "Nooo!" He thrashed and punched. His ban-
dages slipped but the injuries didn't matter. He ran
around the room, sweeping papers off the desk,
kicking chairs yanking books off shelves. He took
a framed still life and crashed it over his own head.
Glass now circled his neck like a death collar.

"Code Red! Code Red!" Dr. Carlson screamed into
the phone.

He tried to grab the frame but Abe swiped him off
like a fly. Suddenly, Abe buckled and fell to the floor,
the glass jabbing into his neck. He felt all his muscles
go limp. His face slackened into a sad smile.

CHAPTER SEVENTEEN

Abe awoke in a different room dimly lit. It was small—his the only bed—and its door had a wired glass window the size of a shoebox. He felt woozy and sore. His head throbbed. What time was it? What had happened? He tried to sit up. He couldn't, his bed rattling. His arms and ankles had been strapped to the metal side bars. The IV had been reinserted. A brace now circled his neck, his skin beneath pulled tight in places with stitches and bandaging.

Abe roared, rattled the bed again, and fell back in defeat.

Sometime later, familiar voices came to him. George and Dr. Carlson were arguing on the other side of his door.

"Not again!" George stated. "He's too far gone now. He might never come back whole."

"We can't stop now. We need to know the truth," Dr. Carlson replied. "The kid believes he killed his mother and sister. We can't leave this unresolved."

That's right, Abe recalled, guilt ripping into him. But there was no "resolving." How could there be? He couldn't bring them back to life, no matter how many therapy sessions he'd attend.

Through the window, George made eye contact with Abe. Dr. Carlson unlocked the door, and both men came into the room.

"What's going on?" Abe rumbled. "Where am I?"

Dr. Carlson said, "You're in a locked room, Abe, and under suicide watch. You were very dangerous yesterday. Do you remember?"

"Yeah, it's coming clear. Hope I didn't hurt anybody. Sorry. I was out of control."

"Till I stuck you with some Haldol, that is. Abe... your father and I have been discussing whether to continue this kind of therapy."

George spoke up. "I don't think it's healthy. You're opening parts of your life that hurt too much. There's nothing you can do to fix—"

"That's not true," Dr. Carlson interrupted. "Abe can learn how to respond to these memories in more helpful ways. Besides, most any therapy—Cognitive Behavioral, for instance—would have him confront his problems too."

George blew out a big breath. "Abe, what do you think?"

He couldn't escape what he had done. It was hard to think straight. Abe closed his eyes and nearly fell asleep again. He barely heard George say, "We'll let you get some more rest, Abe. I'll see you this afternoon."

Woozy, Abe waved a finger.

Hours later, Woody brought in breakfast. He roused Abe by raising the head of the bed to a sitting position.

"I gotta take a leak first," Abe said. "Let me out."

"Sorry, no can do," Woody said. "I can unstrap your arms, but you'll have to piss in this bottle. Better than a catheter, ain't it?"

Still Abe felt like a freaking baby.

Woody got rid of the urine and returned with sanitary wipes for Abe's hands. Then he leaned against the wall and said, "Eat up. I can't go anywhere until you're done with breakfast and I can remove the tray."

Abe picked up the plastic spoon. "Huh!" He dug in because he was hungry, but he barely tasted the food. His stomach felt wrung out. Yesterday's revelations sickened him. James or not, he was a monster and didn't deserve to have freedom, to have people trying to help him. *I should be locked up and tied down for the rest of my life,* he groaned inside.

Late in the morning, Dr. Carlson stopped in to discuss the therapy. "Your dad finally said it was up to you whether we do another session. And if you do want to go through with this, George wants to be present. But he can't do that without your permission."

"I don't want to go back there, Doctor. I don't want to know what else I did."

Dr. Carlson held a hand up. "Please listen first and then decide, Abe. This session is different. You will keep your eyes open and, yes, retell that day all over again."

Frustrated and frightened, Abe bit down on his lips to keep from crying.

"Don't get upset, now. Wait 'til I finish explaining. This time, you make an effort to tell of any good things that day."

"'Good things?' You gotta be kidding."

"No, they're there too, Abe, along with the bad

memories. For instance, you could have noticed the fragrance of a flower, or remembered a joke someone told."

Abe squeezed his temples. "What if I go berzerk again?"

"I've upped your sedative and anti-depressant," Dr. Carlson said. "The higher doses should keep you calmer. We'll keep your IV in."

"I don't know," Abe admitted. "The hand tapping was weird. Being touched—I didn't like that."

"That's okay. We don't have to do it that way. So think about it for a while, and we'll see what happens at three."

After lunch had come and gone, Abe found himself sort of missing the crew at group therapy. He wondered how long he'd be secluded with no visitors. Niko couldn't even visit. Monica. How did Niko's talk with her go? Abe felt so lonely. Woody had wheeled in a TV on a cart, and set it on ESPN. But Abe was bored with teams he had no loyalty for. Plus they put the stupidest sports coverage on during these soap opera hours. Curling, right. Synchronized ice skating, right. He surfed a while, but kept coming across scenes of war—the news on CNN, a talk show on Fox, reruns of "Band of Brothers" on twenty different channels. There was no escaping it. He turned the warring off. But there was no escaping the footage playing again and again in his head. Sleep didn't help much, but it was the only thing he could do right now....

Dr. Carlson was untying Abe's arms restraints when he woke up.

"Hello, Abe."

"Hey."

"Here's some water," Dr. Carlson said, placing a styrofoam cup and plastic pitcher on the swinging tray table. "Those meds can give you wicked dry mouth."

"Thanks."

"What did you decide about another EMDR session?"

"Let's do it," Abe stated, his thumb up. "I want some answers."

"And do you want George to stay?"

George held out his hands in a plea. "Abe, I should be here to help."

"I know you want to help, but...maybe that's part of my problem. You, Vanessa, Niko, have all been so good to me. Doing everything for me. I think it's about time I do something on my own."

"Sure, Abe, if that's what you want," George said quietly. "But I'm going to stand right out here in the hall in case you need me."

"Good enough," Abe said.

Dr. Carlson piped up, "And George, Abe, I promise I'll stop the session if I feel it's becoming dangerous."

"Thanks," George said, and left the room.

"There, young man," Dr. Carlson said, "Let's get going. Since you don't want to be touched, I'd like you to tap these two tongue depressors against your tray. Drum one beat with each hand—back and forth. And follow that beat with your eyes too. That okay?"

"That's cool. I can do that."

"Good, Abe. Now take a deep breath—"

"It hurts my ribs."

"Sorry," Dr. Carlson said, "stupid of me.... Okay, relax, Abe. Let your shoulders melt into the bed, and let out all the tension. You're in a safe place. Everyone here wants the best for you. Now...we're going to focus on the simplest things that made any minute of life worthwhile that day. If only for a few seconds, you smiled. Now, start with the very first thing you did that morning. How did you wake up?"

Abe pictured himself in the kids' area of lean-to's. He'd been lying on a flattened cardboard box, and had slept well. "Smells, good smells woke me up. Meat. Chicken, I think. I hadn't eaten meat in months. But when I went to the kitchen, Grant said only the officers could eat the chicken. We got the regular dumboy. Maybe that was a good thing, because if I had to give meat to the older soldiers, I'd be too tempted to eat it all. Then I would have gotten my hands chopped off!"

"Yes, that's right—that's a very good thing."

"After we cleaned up, I walked down to the pit—"

"The pit? What was that?"

"It's where we went to, you know, take a crap. It was just a deep hole. You could piss any old place, but you had to crap in the pit."

"Okay, remember, Abe, these incidents are supposed to be positive—"

"It *was* positive because a Gio kid was showing a Khran how to squat over it, and the Khran fell back into the pit! It was so funny. All I could see was this head and arms and legs sticking out of this hole! I helped him after a while." Abe hung his head, trying to hide a smile. "Actually, first I got a bunch of other guys to come and see. Then we helped him out."

"That's pretty good," Carlson said with a chuckle. "See, Abe, that day—like every day of your life—is full of all kinds of emotions you have to deal with and respond to. It's amazing how, even in dark times, we find some relief in humor."

"Well, I think that was the end of the humor for that day," Abe said.

"Okay, let's get back into it."

Abe recounted the hand-to-hand drills again. "One kid went too far with the sparring and actually kicked a man in his nuts. This big guy doubled over in agony, and the kid ran off."

"And that's a positive memory because...?"

"Maybe the man had been teasing the kid like the big Khran did to me. Maybe it was pay-back, you know?"

"I see what you're saying," Dr. Carlson said. "However, violence isn't the best response to violence. Now, you'd told me that Grant had seen what the big Khran soldier was doing to you. Where did you run to finally? Your lean-to?"

"I didn't run to Grant, if that's what you're thinking. It was raining, so I sneaked inside the factory and hid among the machines. I could see my mother. Ellie was at her side. That was good. They were mending clothes. It made me laugh a little because Mom was always sewing up my ripped pants or darning a sock at home. She saved all her mending for rainy days. We'd crowd up our kitchen, and try to 'help' her. Ellie and I played games with the buttons. We'd see who could build the tallest tower before it fell. We played button soccer on the table."

Dr. Carlson's eyes crinkled. "See, some of the good things from Liberia survived all that horror. You preserved those memories and carried them like treasures into your current life."

"You're right," Abe said, tilting his head. "And it's little stuff like that—little details—that I miss, too."

Abe hated to disturb the sweet moment, but Dr. Carlson prodded him to continue. Abe retold about waking to the sounds of fist-fighting. How he'd enjoyed watching the Khran man die.

"After Grant gave me the pills, we had some free time. I went back to the lean-to. I lay there daydreaming about what Mom, Ellie and I would do once the fighting ended. We were going to buy a small fishing boat, and live closer to the water. We'd be rich from selling all the fish we caught. And we'd never be hungry. I didn't want to go back to our neighborhood. I would have died if I had to see that school and the burned out homes. And if the war started again, we could just sail away from it, to a place where nobody was fighting anybody. Stupid dreams," Abe muttered.

"Not at all, Abe," Dr. Carlson said. "What child would want to stay in a war zone? What child wouldn't dream of someplace better, a haven?"

Abe shrugged.

"After a while, a kid came in and told me that the Gio kids were going to have a soccer game against the Khran boys. Somebody had made a ball out of rags. We played the rest of the afternoon in the warm rain. I scored twice. ...I had forgotten about that! Slipping and diving in the mud, and running around. I didn't even know who won. It didn't matter."

"You got to play, like children are supposed to," Dr. Carlson stated.

Abe recalled that he ate potatoes for dinner. "And there was milk! Goat's milk—from a farm nearby. Some soldiers had stolen the goats—led them to the factory. Everybody wanted to eat the goats, but Grant told them having the milk supply was better. I bet my mother would have to milk the goats. I pictured her doing it and I laughed. She'd never milked anything before. But she did nurse me and Ellie. Maybe that counted for experience."

The doctor gave Abe a small smile, and pointed at the tongue depressors.

"Don't stop the beat, Abe. What happened after dinner?"

"I took another one of the pills Grant had given to me. It made my heart go really fast, and made me feel strong. When my mom called me 'son,' my heart felt like a feather and my head tingled. I was happy I could help them escape. And the guard I distracted, he was a pretty good guy."

"Then came the shots and screams," Dr. Carlson prodded. "Remember now, search for something positive."

"I don't think I can, Doctor," Abe said, stopping his sticks. "It's too horrible."

"Try, Abe, this is the really important part. Open your eyes, keep tapping and try!"

"Okay!" Abe picked up the pace of the beat. "I saw Mom and Ellie being led to that corner room, so that's good, right? Or else I wouldn't have known where they were."

"Yes, that's right."

"And I guess the loaded rifles leaning against the wall—that was lucky because I just grabbed one, and it was ready to fire."

"If the guns were across the room, Abe, the soldiers would have gotten to them in time. They would have killed you."

Abe nodded, startled how things could make sense. "I fired before anybody could move, really. And when Grant came, it was good that he didn't have a lot of men, because I probably wouldn't have gotten them all."

"And your mother and sister?"

The tapping quickened. Abe's voice rose. "There were men lying all around, I could barely see Ellie—maybe they weren't shot at all, or maybe not shot too bad. But I still don't remember my mom and my sister moving, Doctor." Abe's mouth went dry and the words stopped coming out. The tapping was rolling—a high pitched repetition on the tray, a rolling drum on a snare.

The doctor lifted the water cup to Abe's mouth. Abe gulped it like it was his last drink on Earth.

"Now look at me again, Abe," Dr. Carlson demanded. "We're not done. Your mom and Ellie—were they bleeding? Bring that picture to mind, Abe. Picture James, like you're watching a movie unfold. Focus hard!"

Abe searched his mind for fragments of that scene. "There was so much blood—everywhere...." He zeroed in on his mother's housedress, faded gray from months of wear. He couldn't see any of the yellow flowers that used to be in the print. But he did see red.

"But only a little blood on my mom!" he blurted. "A smear, at the left side of my mom's waist where the man had rolled off her. And Ellie...." Abe's eyes rolled skyward, picturing his sister. "Just drops of blood on her bare legs, nothing higher. Maybe she was wounded, or maybe it came from the soldiers. I don't know. And then Grant came and I killed him."

"And you got satisfaction from that," Dr. Carlson said.

"Yes! For everything he did to me and Steven! For everything he did to my mother and sister! I was glad I killed him!"

"Where did you go? There must have been soldiers rushing to the scene with all that gunfire. But obviously you escaped."

"Yeah, I ran toward the area where my mom and Ellie had tried to escape. Because most of those soldiers guarding the area were probably in the room dead. I ran and ran through the woods, the guns were heavy. I stopped to rest a moment and to listen. The soldiers' hollering was still far off. But there! A faint crackle. I sat as still as the trees, my gun pointing at the noise. I looked through the gun sight, and it got magnified. I saw people—two of them—running. A grown-up and a smaller person, maybe a child."

"A child?"

"Maybe. Could it be?" Abe asked hopefully. He wanted to believe so much.

"Hold that picture, Abe! Make it concrete now with details. Think of their clothes."

"Their legs were bare—they shined in the moonlight a bit. So it wouldn't have been soldiers in their long pants. These people had skirts or dresses. And the small one was carrying something. Something sort of bright."

"Food? Clothing? A weapon of some sort?" the doctor suggested.

Abe's sticks raced. He closed one eye as if peering through a gun sight. "It was pink—a rag. Bunny! It was Ellie's! It had to be Ellie and Mom! Dr. Carlson, they were alive!"

"Did you go to them?"

"I wanted to, so bad, but if the soldiers searched for me and found me with Mom and Ellie, they'd kill them too. They'd probably make *me* kill them. They liked to do that—get the kids to kill their own families. But I didn't do it, I didn't kill them. I maybe even helped them get away."

Abe's aching chest heaved and tears sprang from

his eyes. He threw the tongue depressors in the air and grabbed Dr. Carslon in a painful bear hug. "I didn't kill them! I didn't kill them! I didn't, I didn't!"

CHAPTER EIGHTEEN

Abe's euphoria lasted only the few minutes he spent in George's arms, after he was let inside the room. Dr. Carlson was pacing the hall outside the door, and suddenly Abe knew why.

"George," he said, "Can you go get Dr. Carlson?"

"Sure, son," he said, drying his own tears. "Anything you want."

The men returned together.

"Yes, Abe?" Dr. Carlson asked.

Abe cleared his throat. "I remember when we first started this EMDR stuff, that sometimes it's hard to tell if the patient is telling the truth, or saying only what he wants to believe."

Dr. Carlson folded his arms across his chest. "Yes, Abe," he said quietly, "that's true."

Abe stared into George's eyes. He looked hurt and disappointed all over again, the way he had looked in the locker room that time Abe had elbowed him in the face.

Abe glanced back at Dr. Carlson and said, "There's got to be a way we can find out if it's true. Or else it could never be...resolved. Is that the right word?"

George squeezed Abe's forearm. "Yes! Abe, in the refugee camp, the Red Cross was working on family reunification. They couldn't find your family then. Maybe your mom and Ellie hadn't reached a camp yet, or any camp at all."

Dr. Carlson nodded, saying, "Let's not get our hopes up wildly, people. Over the next few days, Abe will repeat and repeat his story. The accuracy of the details will help us determine if he's telling the truth."

Abe crossed his fingers and prayed there would be no other "truth."

"In the meantime, Abe, if you and your father wish to search for news of your family, go right ahead. But remember, fighting has continued off and on in Liberia all these years. Your mother and sister could have perished in another conflict."

Abe hung his head. How unjust it would be if he had saved them, only to have them die anyway.

Two days and positive therapy sessions later, Abe moved back to a regular room on the ward floor. He was free of the IV tether and could go to the bathroom on his own, thank God. Two days later, the suicide watch had been lifted. And he was allowed to have immediate family visitors again.

After dinner, Abe was called to the visitors' room. "You have company," the nurse informed him. Abe steeled himself to meet Vanessa. He had no idea what to expect from her, no clue what to say.

Niko, instead, waited for Abe through the glassed-in supervisor's room.

"Hey, dog," Niko said, doing this bobbing and weaving thing.

A good start, Abe thought. George said he'd filled everybody in on the latest mental health news. Seemed like Niko believed Abe wasn't going to hack him to death.

"Welcome back to my crib," Abe said, slapping Niko's hand. "Not as nice as Club Elders, I must admit."

"Yeah," said Niko. "Doesn't have that homeplace feel. Doesn't look like a guy could put a fist through these walls either."

Niko sat, stretching his legs the length of the couch.

"Give me some room, bro," Abe said, shoving Nik's huge Converse-clad feet to the floor. "What's going on in the real world?"

Niko bragged, "I blew away the school record again in shot put."

"Sweet!" Abe said, knocking knuckles. "Catch any hurdles action?"

"Yeah, you know, Khalid's wiping up the conference."

Abe smirked. "Figures."

"Yeah, so what, you'll whup his ass in the outdoor season," Niko said, sitting up straight.

"Word is, I can't compete, but I'd like to work out with the team and get back in shape."

"You've gone flabby and soft, all this pampering."

A big question hovered in the air like a blimp. Abe had hoped that Niko would just volunteer the information, but Niko wasn't always the quickest on the uptake.

"So...how did things go with Monica?"

"Shitty—what did you expect?"

Abe shrugged. "I didn't expect anything. I never broke up with anybody before."

"Take it from the pro, here," Niko replied. "Her chin

was all wobbly, and her eyes were filling up. But she held it together pretty good."

"That's Monica," Abe said quietly. "She say anything?"

"Not at first. But this morning I found this note shoved in my locker."

Abe grabbed for it, but Niko pulled it away. "Come on, it's mine."

"It was in *my* locker."

"You A-hole."

"Here," Niko said. "Take it. I already read the sorry-ass letter anyway."

Abe gave Niko a sharp elbow.

"Oww!" Nik complained. "You go on and be that way, dog. See if I do any more favors for you."

> *Dear Abe,*
> *I know you're thinking you're doing the*
> *right thing. I respect that. All I ask is, when*
> *you're feeling better, give me a call. I'm not*
> *waiting around—you understand—I got a lot of*
> *things to do. But I know enough of you to know*
> *I'd like more. That's all.*
> *love, Moan ee cah*

Choked up, Abe folded the letter.

"Aww, man," Niko said, "You ain't going all Niagara Falls on me, are you?"

Just then, the supervisor's voice came through. "Your mother is on the phone, Abe."

"My mother!?" Abe jumped.

The nurse added, "She wants to know if it's okay to stop in."

"Ohhh." He sank back into the couch. "It's Vanessa."

Niko cocked his head and whispered, "Talk to her, man. It's been real hard for her."

Hard for her? Abe called, "Can you tell her I have a guest? Maybe she could try again tomorrow around lunch."

"What did you do that for?" Niko asked.

"How long have I been in here—about ten days? Well, she only visited once and that was because George dragged her in. She's got some serious problem with me, and I'm not ready to talk to her about it yet. Maybe tomorrow."

Later in bed, Abe outlined a plan of action. If Vanessa pulls a "I go or you go" scene, Abe would move out, of course. He couldn't break up George's family like that. His eighteenth birthday was in two weeks. He could get a decent job, maybe go part-time to college. Save up enough money to bring Ellie and his mother over. Abe focused on his mother's face when she last called him "son." He longed to see her again, the high proud cheek bones, the rock-steady brown eyes. He had to hear from those agencies soon. She had to turn up somewhere.

After a good night's sleep, Abe decided to go to the hospital chapel for Sunday service. Woody escorted him down to the first floor. He even sat next to Abe in the pew.

Having an escort now was overkill, Abe thought, musing on the word itself. He didn't feel like a danger to himself or to others anymore. That urge to strike had faded. Hopefully forever, with the doctor's help.

Abe prayed silently, "God, sometimes I feel like Job with all the bad stuff that's been thrown at me. Yet I still believe in You and I want to do the right things from now on. Ease up on me, okay? And please keep

George and Vanessa, Niko, and Monica safe and healthy. Especially, let us find Mom and Ellie alive and well. Thanks, Big Guy."

After communion, Abe spotted Vanessa in the back row. She gave him a little wave and a pale smile. The service soon ended, and Woody led Abe to the back of the room.

"Hello, Abe," she said, a bit shaky.

"Is it okay if Vanessa here comes upstairs with us for a visit?" he asked Woody.

"Yeah, sure," he said. "Mrs. Elders, we'll just have to sign you in."

In silence, they rode the elevator then went through the ward paperwork. Woody unlocked the visitors' room, and took a seat in the supervisor booth.

"My mouth is so dry, I can barely speak, Abe," Vanessa said finally. She took a bottle of water from her purse and offered it to Abe first. "Want a sip?"

"No, thanks," Abe replied, sitting on one end of the couch.

She heaved a sigh and said, "I decided not to tell you I was going to visit this morning. That way you couldn't say 'no,' or 'not now' or even...'never.'"

Abe shrugged.

"You'd think I'd have all the right words—I counsel families day in and day out at work. But...um."

"I know," Abe said. "This whole thing freaks me out too."

Vanessa admitted, "I'm sorry I didn't come see you. I just couldn't. I've helped ex-cons in my life, no problem. Husbands who beat their wives, no problem. But when it's my own...son...who killed with or without cause, I couldn't face it." She dabbed at her eyes with a handkerchief.

Abe had no answer. He started sweating, dreading the painful words to come. Vanessa hadn't even touched him, much less given him kiss or a pat on the back. As if she'd catch whatever disease he had. She had come to him only to distance herself. To make the distance permanent. He felt it as concretely as the table separating them.

"I'll be eighteen soon," Abe stated. "I can get my own place, a job."

Vanessa's hands dropped into her lap. "What?"

"As soon as they discharge me, I can leave the house."

"Abe, nobody is throwing you out," Vanessa said.

Abe shrugged. "It sure feels like it. So, I'll just leave on my own. You don't have to spell it out for me."

Her eyes brimming, Vanessa walked around the table and cupped Abe's face. "Spell *this* out: I L-o-v-e Y-o-u. I came here to beg forgiveness from *you*. And to promise I will never leave you in a time of pain again."

"Really?" asked, his body suddenly weightless.

She hugged his head to her. "Forever, I promise."

And he wrapped his arms around her.

CHAPTER NINETEEN

Ten days later, Dr. Carlson discharged Abe from the hospital. He was sure— and so was Abe—that he hadn't killed his family. He had even helped them escape. Now the mission of finding his mother and sister filled Abe's every new minute with hope and agonizing suspense. Every phone call could be the one he prayed for.

On Holy Thursday morning, it came at 5am. Knowing Liberia is four hours ahead, Abe jumped to answer it. The connection was horrible and he strained to hear the words.

"This is Leeza Stack from the Red Cross in Monrovia."

"Yes!" Abe's eyes swept across the expectant faces of Vanessa, Niko and George.

"We have no record that a Mrs. Mary Odo or a Miss Eleanor Odo had ever lived in refugee camps the Red Cross operates in West Africa."

Abe's mouth fell open and he lost his breath.

"Hello? Is somebody there?" cackled over the phone.

Abe dropped the phone to his side and almost turned the power off. George leaped to the phone and shouted, "Hello! Yes, this is Dr. George Elders.... I see.... Oh, that's a good idea. Thank you."

Abe had sunk into his seat and placed his head on the table. He felt lifeless. Niko rubbed his shoulders and Vanessa held his hand.

"Abe," George said. "Listen—there are other ways to find them. The Red Cross lady said to get a list of hospitals in Liberia—there are barely any, Abe—and check the hospitals near border areas in the surrounding countries. Plus we haven't heard back from the U.S. Embassy yet either. So don't despair, Abe. We're not done hunting by a long shot."

Abe lifted his head and rubbed his face. "Okay. We keep trying."

"Good," George said. "After practice today, you two get an atlas and hit the internet. Find those hospitals and have them search their records. I'll get back on the diplomacy route. I don't have to show at the hospital until 2 pm tomorrow. And you guys are off tomorrow for Good Friday. We can get a lot done if we wake up early."

By the time Abe and Niko arrived at school, Abe had regained his energy. He didn't give a damn who said what about whatever at school. He had achieved some normalcy and it felt great. Even Mrs. Blalock waved to him in the hall. And Abe, in his new world of forgiveness, waved back.

After school, Abe walked down to the track. They officially started outdoor practice March first. Abe loved it when the season changed. Running in clean fresh air beat an indoor track hands down. Indoors, dust coated your tongue and throat. Outdoors, track was like playing tag on a summer day.

Still in his school clothes, he spotted Khalid setting up the last of the hurdles. Abe didn't feel one ounce of tension eyeing his rival. Funny how things fall into better perspective once you've climbed up from hell.

"Abe!" Khalid said. "Hey, man, you okay now? Gonna get back into the starting blocks? I've been missing you."

"Yeah, right," Abe chuckled.

"Truth! We can't go one-two in the hurdles without you, and our relay sucked since you left. When can you go all out again?"

"I'm ready up here," Abe said pointing to his head. Then he motioned to his right side, and added, "But I still have another four weeks to go here. Plus months more of physical therapy."

"Sheeeet," Khalid said.

"Seen Coach yet?"

"Yeah, he's around."

Abe surveyed the track. Sprinters, including Monica, were running up and down the bleachers while the hurdlers got in their track workout. The distance runners had taken off for a warm-up run in the neighborhood. And there was Niko flinging his javelin on the soccer field. He was chasing the school record in discus, too. Abe would have to supervise Niko's training at home. Niko had cut back on partying, but he was still a lazy ass. Think how good he could be if he really gave 100 percent.

Abe spotted Coach near the jumpers.

"Abe!" Coach said, shaking Abe's hand. "It's great to have you back. How ya feeling?"

Abe gave Coach the timetable for his recovery.

"Then you're okay for leg workouts in the meantime?"

"Yup!" Abe said. He couldn't wait to exercise hard and sweat again. The exercises and equipment at the hospital were lame.

"Okay, back to the weight room for you, but go easy. Give me ten minutes on the stairs machine, ten minutes hamstring curls, ten minutes of quad extensions. Low weights, high reps. And do a full ten minute stretch before you start and after you're done."

"Great!" Abe said, grinning like a kid going to the circus.

"Oh, Abe, see me in my office after practice. I have to talk to you about college."

Well, that deflated him. As he walked back toward the gym, Abe wondered what had happened on the scholarship front. What Division 1 school would invest in a nutcase? He didn't feel like one anymore. He was meeting with Dr. Carlson once a week. And weekly group wasn't all that bad. He'd made friends with a few vets—including two women—from the Gulf Wars. He had more in common with the young vets. Maybe in a few years, Abe could be a group facilitator.

In the locker room, Abe sat at the bench in front of his locker. He stared, confounded, at the combination lock. What was it? He had easily opened his school locker. That combo had been seared into his brain over four years. Wait. Just think. Right—the day numbers of Niko's birthday, spin to the left until Vanessa's day, and back to the right for Doc's. He smiled to think how closely he was knitted into this family.

Abe's abbreviated workout ended before the rest of the team's, so he got to pick out the best shower head in the locker room. His feet slid across the slimy tiled floor, reminding him of the bottom of Sidman's Cove, where he and Steven went swimming.

"Steven," Abe thought. Maybe he should try to commune with people who had died. "Steven, you there? Um, well, how you doing in Heaven? I'm not in any hurry to join you anymore, but save me a seat."

Suddenly the hot water went cold. "Yi!" Abe yipped. Looking upward, he laughed. That was a good one!

As the rest of the team came in, Abe met up with Coach. He signaled to close the door as he sat behind his desk. "I'm going to be upfront with you, Abe. The recruiters from Rutgers, UCONN, and Temple have stopped asking about you."

"Yeah, I figured," Abe said, blowing air out the side of his mouth. "Did they even ask what happened?"

"Yes, and of course I didn't say anything specific—I just said 'medical problems.' But when they saw you not showing up meet after meet, they pretty much counted you out. And now that you're so-so about the outdoor season....I'm sorry, Abe."

"That's okay. I appreciate everything you've done for me, Coach. I'm going to talk with my family and see what's best. To tell you the truth, after all this, I'm not up for living too far from home. But I thought maybe Towson State or George Washington...?"

"They're not power players, but let me see what I can do," Coach said.

That night, Niko didn't go out. "I'm spending it right here with my brother," he explained. "Let's hit those hospitals."

"I'll do the Liberian and Ivory Coast ones on Doc's laptop, you check Sierra Leone, and Guinea." Abe shivered. All those countries except Guinea had been embroiled in their own civil wars. Wasn't there any safe place in the world?

The boys rose at 5 am Friday—9 am in West Africa—

and got right to work on the phones. They'd spent last night getting the telephone numbers of eighty-three different hospitals across four countries. Hopefully, Abe's mom and Ellie had shown up someplace!

They soon learned how futile their plan was. Most of the hospitals in the Ivory Coast and Sierra Leone had only spotty records. Fighting and looting had damaged or burned the facilities. Niko had better luck in Guinea, which had managed to remain neutral. Non-government organizations had used Guinea as a host for refugee camps and peace talks. There were also more English-speaking employees there.

Around eight, Niko said, "I'm starving! I'm not used to functioning this early. How about a couple of bagels?"

"Sounds good," Abe said, standing to stretch. "I'll go get them, and start a pot of coffee."

"Make mine an everything bagel with cream cheese," Niko bellowed.

Downstairs, Vanessa already had the coffee maker going. She didn't have the day off. "It's going to be a good day, Abraham Elders. I can feel it!"

Abe smiled. "I hope so. It's so frustrating not knowing anything for sure."

"I know, but life is like that for everybody. We just have to increase our knowledge and our love and deal with what life gives us. You happened to have gotten a bigger share of sorrowful events. But you're due for some good news."

That's the old Vanessa, Abe thought. Upbeat and fearless—not the weak and wooden Vanessa he saw last month.

"I got it! I got it!" Niko hollered. Vanessa, Abe and George stampeded into the rec room. "Conakry! They were in the hospital in Conakry," Niko said, holding his hand over the mouthpiece. "They're checking the dates now."

"Let Abe have the phone, Nik," George said. "They won't release information to a non-relative."

Abe took the phone as if it were a crown of jewels. "Hello? This is Abraham Eld—I mean Abraham Odo. I'm looking for information about my mother Mary Odo and my sister Eleanor Odo."

"Yes. We show no patient record of an Eleanor Odo."

Abe felt weak. He couldn't take any more bad news.

"We did have a Mary Odo, who was a patient several years ago."

Abe gasped. "How can I find her? I must find her! Is there an address?"

"I'm very sorry to tell you, Mr. Odo, but Mary Odo died of malaria."

"Malaria?" Abe buckled and fell to his knees. Vanessa and Niko huddled around him.

George clicked on the speaker phone. "Hello, this is Dr. George Elders in Maryland. I'm the adoptive father of Abraham Odo. Do your records show a 'next of kin?'"

"Yes, sir, it is Eleanor Odo."

"That means she's alive?"

Abe lifted his eyes to George.

"Well, sir, all I can say is that she was alive at the time of Mary Odo's death."

"Is there a phone number or address for Eleanor Odo?"

"Yes, sir, the local number in Conakry is 88-452. It is the St. Theresa orphanage.

"Thank you very much," said George and they disconnected. He hugged Abe from behind. "I'm so sorry about your mother, Abe." George looked skyward and yelled, "Haven't You punished him enough?"

Abe couldn't believe it. *Malaria*? How many mosquito bites had he gotten and scratched until they festered? One bug, one bite, and she was gone from him. She'd worked too hard to be killed by one bug. She pulled Ellie through. In her stubbornness, she pulled Abe through too. She'd kept him returning to her, kept him wanting her love, inspired him to save them. At least for a while.

After a few moments, George asked, "Abe, are you ready to try the orphanage?"

Abe nodded. They left the speaker on and punched in the numbers. The sound of an accent so like his own lifted Abe's heart. The receptionist transferred them to an office worker. Another similar accent. She introduced herself as Sister Marlene.

"Records for Eleanor Odo? Ellie, of course! We placed her last year with a family back in her old neighborhood. We were sad to see her go—she was a big help with the little ones—why, she—"

"Number?" Abe croaked.

George said, "Yes, may we please have the number and the name for the family? Please, this is urgent."

"Certainly, let me pull her file...."

Rustlings and bangs and squeaky chair noises came through the speaker. Niko rolled his eyes and did a whisper-shout, "Come on already, Nun!!"

Sister Marlene came back and gave them the number. Niko scribbled it down and shut off the phone.

"Niko!" Abe hollered. "The name, we missed the name!"

"Sorry! I'm just so excited! We'll find out the name soon enough, like now."

"Who do you think took her in, Abe?" George asked. "Cousins? Family friends?"

Abe shook his head. "My mother and father were only children. We didn't have any cousins. And after my father died, we broke off from his political friends. They were dangerous to be seen with."

While George dialed again and waited for the international operator, Niko shouted, "What about that friend your mom and Ellie were escaping to? Think hard, Abe!"

My mother's friends? He'd lost that slip of paper soon after he got it.

Vanessa asked, "Your neighbors, school mates? Try hard to remember."

Abe pictured his old school with its clean white walls and chalk-filled blackboards, he heard children chanting multiplication tables and singing folk songs. His mind's eye flowed down the hall to caf and now saw camouflaged men with guns, and he remembered him and Steven screaming inside the empty pails.

"Steven?" Abe whispered.

"Got it!" George shouted. It rang once, twice, then a girl's voice came through.

"El-Ellie?" Abe stammered. Tears sprang from his eyes.

"Yes? This is Ellie. Who's this?"

"It's me, Ellie. It's Abe."

"Abe? Abe!" she screamed. Joy and shock blared through the speaker. "Is it really you? Oh Abe! God in Heaven! Where are you?"

"I'm here in America! Where are you?"

"With the Pearls, Steven's mom—his dad and two older brothers are gone, and," Ellie's voice grew quiet, "you know about Steven, of course."

"Of course, Ellie," said Abe. "I think of him every day."

Ellie's voice sounded cautious. "And you, Abe, are you all right?"

Abe's eyes journeyed over the faces of Niko, Vanessa, George. He gathered them into his arms and answered, "I'm better now, Ellie. I'm so much better. And I can't wait to hug you. I will, very soon."

AFTERWORD and ACKNOWLEDGEMENTS

Having been a child during the Vietnam War and involved in humanitarian efforts very young in my reli-
gious community, I have always been sensitive to war's
impact on children. I saw it firsthand when I visited
a refugee camp in Thailand in 1989. I had just started to write for children and felt that young readers
needed to know about injustices done to their peers
around the world. My books with themes of children's
rights include *The Whispering Cloth: A Refugee's
Story*; *Tangled Threads: A Hmong Girl's Story*; and *The
Carpet Boy's Gift* about child labor in Pakistan.

Liberia specifically came into my ken in the latter
part of 1990 when I was glued to CNN for news about
the Iraqi invasion of Kuwait. My brother Tommie
Deitz, a Navy SEAL commander, had been dispatched
immediately to the area (and soon became a hero
whose exploits are now legendary in the Navy). At the
same time, CNN was covering the civil war re-igniting
in Liberia. Being the daughter of a history teacher, I
got out my atlas, read up on the country, and began
following its politics.

Several years later, a refugee family from Liberia moved into our neighborhood in Rockville, CT. The Bestmans had children the same ages as mine, so we carpooled, did birthday parties, etc. They allowed me to interview them and to publish a magazine article about them in *Footsteps: African American History* (Jan/Feb 2001, volume 3, number 1). I'll never forget Mrs. Ruth Bestman's great fear of the boy soldiers, enslaved, trained and drugged by adult militias to kill. I expanded my research on child labor to include this horrific development, and found that it had been occurring all over the world for centuries. Whereas child soldiers used to be a last resort (as in the American Civil War), now children were being pushed *ahead* of the front line as human mine sweepers, spraying bullets with AK-47s as big as themselves. If these children survived physically, how could they possibly resume normal lives?

I would like to acknowledge many people for helping me understand the lifelong damage bourn by child soldiers and child "brides" (young girls who were kidnapped and sexually enslaved by adult soldiers). First and foremost, thank you to the Bestman family for allowing me to probe their most agonizing memories to bring awareness to this issue. I am indebted to Dr. Eleanor Pershing of the West Africa Trauma Team, who worked with groups in Sierra Leone and Liberia to counsel children, build schools and rehabilitate child soldiers. She and others in their Indiana community have also hosted and/or adopted and rehabilitated Liberian boys here in the U.S. I received valuable information and manuscript critique from Dr. Pershing, and also from Christina Lee of Catholic Relief Services. Ms. Lee, Peace Building Program

Manager, worked in rehabilitating and educating young soldiers in four sectors across Uganda. My love and gratitude to Susan Kalkhuis-Beam who worked in war refugee services for years in Thailand and in Bosnia. And to Ferdinand Kalkhuis, one of the first relief workers in Rwanda and its bordering countries during the genocide of 1994, and who has also served in Bosnia and Kosovo. I am grateful to Father Justinian Rweyemamu of Tanzania and Connecticut for his thoughts, prayers and support.

I would also like to thank Dr. Lisa Karabelnik, Dr. Stephen Polesel, and Dr. David Tolin for their expertise regarding post traumatic stress disorder, in- and out-patient psychiatric care, pharmacology, EMDR, cognitive-behavioral therapy and other treatments.

Lastly, I thank the members of the Wednesday Writers Group (who meet on Tuesday) for helping me craft this brutal material. Hopefully this story will help halt the atrocity of child soldiering and make young readers realize the profound toll of violence.

The Real Cost of Prisons Comix

One out of every hundred adults in the U.S. is in prison. This book provides a crash course in what drives mass incarceration, the human and community costs, and how to stop the numbers from going even higher. This volume collects the three comic books published by the Real Cost of Prisons Project—Prison Town: Paying the Price, Prisoners of the War on Drugs, Prisoners of a Hard Life: Women and Their Children.

The stories and statistical information in each comic book is thoroughly researched and documented.

Over 125,000 copies of the comic books have been printed and more than 100,000 have been sent to families of people who are incarcerated, people who are incarcerated, and to organizers and activists throughout the country. The book includes a chapter with descriptions about how the comix have been put to use in the work of organizers and activists in prison and in the "free world" by ESL teachers, high school teachers, college professors, students, and health care providers throughout the country. The demand for them is constant and the ways in which they are being used is inspiring.

Lois Ahrens editor

PM Press

978-1-60486-034-4

104 pages

$12.95

PM PRESS
PO BOX 23912, OAKLAND CA 94623
TEL.: 510-658-3906 • WWW.PMPRESS.ORG

Revolutionary Women: A Book of Stencils

A radical feminist history and street art resource for inspired readers! This book combines short biographies with striking and usable stencil images of thirty women— activists, anarchists, feminists, freedom-fighters and visionaries.

It offers a subversive portrait history which refuses to belittle the military prowess and revolutionary drive of women, whose violent resolves often shatter the archetype of woman-as-nurturer. It is also a celebration of some extremely brave women who have spent their lives fighting for what they believe in and rallying supporters in climates where a woman's authority is never taken as seriously as a man's. The text also shares some of each woman's ideologies, philosophies, struggles and quiet humanity with quotes from their writings or speeches.

Queen of the Neighbourhood

PM Press

978-1-60486-200-3

128 pages

$13.95

PM PRESS
PO BOX 23912, OAKLAND CA 94623
TEL.: 510-658-3906 • WWW.PMPRESS.ORG

Girls Are Not Chicks Coloring Book

Twenty-seven pages of feminist fun! This is a coloring book you will never outgrow. Girls Are Not Chicks *is a subversive and playful way to examine how pervasive gender stereotypes are in every aspect of our lives. This book helps to deconstruct the homogeneity of gender expression in children's media by showing diverse pictures that reinforce positive gender roles for girls.*

Color the Rapunzel for a new society. She now has power tools, a roll of duct tape, a Tina Turner album, and a bus pass!

Paint outside the lines with Miss Muffet as she tells that spider off and considers a career as an arachnologist!

Girls are not chicks. Girls are thinkers, creators, fighters, healers and superheroes.

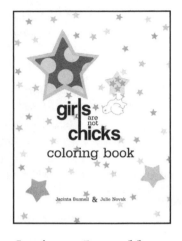

Jacinta Bunnell
and Julie Novak

PM Press &
Reach and Teach

978-1-60486-076-4

32 pages

$10.00

REACH AND TEACH
29 MIRA VISTA COURT, DALY CITY, CA 94014
TEL.: (888) PEACE-40 • WWW.REACHANDTEACH.COM

PM PRESS
PO BOX 23912, OAKLAND CA 94623
TEL.: 510-658-3906 • WWW.PMPRESS.ORG

Sometimes the Spoon Runs Away with Another Spoon Coloring Book

We have the power to change fairy tales and nursery rhymes so that these stories are more realistic. In Sometimes the Spoon Runs Away With Another Spoon you will find anecdotes of real kids' lives and true-to-life fairy tale characters. This book pushes us beyond rigid gender expectations while we color fantastic beasts who like pretty jewelry and princesses who build rocket ships.

Celebrate sensitive boys, tough girls, and others who do not fit into a disempowering gender categorization.

Sometimes the Spoon... aids the work of dismantling the Princess Industrial Complex by moving us forward with more honest representations of our children and ourselves. Color to your heart's content. Laugh along with the characters. Write your own fairy tales. Share your own truths.

Jacinta Bunnell
and Nat Kucinitz

PM Press &
Reach and Teach

978-1-60486-329-1

32 pages

$10.00

REACH AND TEACH
29 MIRA VISTA COURT, DALY CITY, CA 94014
TEL.: (888) PEACE-40 • WWW.REACHANDTEACH.COM

PM PRESS
PO BOX 23912, OAKLAND CA 94623
TEL.: 510-658-3906 • WWW.PMPRESS.ORG

About Reach and Teach

Reach and Teach was launched in 2003 after a High School student told co-founders Craig Wiesner and Derrick Kikuchi "I don't care what you two do for a living, but whatever it is, you should stop. What you need to be doing is what you just did in that classroom—teaching kids like us about what's really going on in the world and what we can do about it." Wiesner and Kikuchi had just shared a presentation about the realities of the war in Afghanistan, realities they had witnessed first hand, carrying home stories they'd promised to tell far and wide. Over 200 students had attended their presentations that day, the day before the U.S. would launch "Shock and Awe," invading Iraq. On that day, the idea for Reach And Teach was born.

Reach And Teach is a peace and social justice learning company, creating and distributing books, CDs, DVDs, curriculum, posters, games, and toys that promote nonviolence, diversity, social and economic justice, and sustaining and healing the planet. As treasure hunters, Reach And Teach is a one stop shop for tools to build a better world through learning. The treasures come from small publishers, non-profit organizations, and social enterprises with products that won't easily find their way into big-box superstores. Through their imprint with PM Press, Reach And Teach creates new treasures, like *Abe in Arms*, which other publishers would not print. "Let other publishers do the books about werewolves and vampires," co-founder Craig Wiesner says. "We'll take on the stories about monsters that really do steal children from their beds at night, and create a new generation of people who take on those monsters and put them in their place."

Reach and Teach
29 Mira Vista Court
Daly City, CA 94014
(888) PEACE-40
www.reachandteach.com

About PM

PM Press was founded at the end of 2007 by a small collection of folks with decades of publishing, media, and organizing experience. PM co-founder Ramsey Kanaan started AK Press as a young teenager in Scotland almost 30 years ago and, together with his fellow PM Press co-conspirators, has published and distributed hundreds of books, pamphlets, CDs, and DVDs. Members of PM have founded enduring book fairs, spearheaded victorious tenant organizing campaigns, and worked closely with bookstores, academic conferences, and even rock bands to deliver political and challenging ideas to all walks of life. We're old enough to know what we're doing and young enough to know what's at stake.

We seek to create radical and stimulating fiction and non-fiction books, pamphlets, t-shirts, visual and audio materials to entertain, educate and inspire you. We aim to distribute these through every available channel with every available technology - whether that means you are seeing anarchist classics at our bookfair stalls; reading our latest vegan cookbook at the café; downloading geeky fiction e-books; or digging new music and timely videos from our website.

PM Press is always on the lookout for talented and skilled volunteers, artists, activists and writers to work with. If you have a great idea for a project or can contribute in some way, please get in touch.

PM Press
PO Box 23912
Oakland CA 94623
510-658-3906
www.pmpress.org

Friends of PM

These are indisputably momentous times—the financial system is melting down globally and the Empire is stumbling. Now more than ever there is a vital need for radical ideas.

In the year since its founding—and on a mere shoestring—PM Press has risen to the formidable challenge of publishing and distributing knowledge and entertainment for the struggles ahead. We have published an impressive and stimulating array of literature, art, music, politics, and culture. Using every available medium, we've succeeded in connecting those hungry for ideas and information to those putting them into practice.

Friends of PM allows you to directly help impact, amplify, and revitalize the discourse and actions of radical writers, filmmakers, and artists. It provides us with a stable foundation from which we can build upon our early successes and provides a much-needed subsidy for the materials that can't necessarily pay their own way.

It's a bargain for you too. For a minimum of $25 a month (we encourage more, needless to say), you'll get all the audio and video (over a dozen CDs and DVDs in our first year) or all of the print (also over a dozen in our first year). Or for $40 you get everything published in hard copy PLUS the ability to purchase any/all items you've missed at a 50% discount. And what could be better than the thrill of receiving a monthly package of cutting edge political theory, art, literature, ideas and practice delivered to your door?

For those who can't afford $25 or more a month, we're introducing Sustainer Rates at $15, $10 and $5. Sustainers get a free PM Press t-shirt and a 50% discount on all purchases from our website.

Your card will be billed once a month, until you tell us to stop. Or until our efforts succeed in bringing the revolution around. Or the financial meltdown of Capital makes plastic redundant. Whichever comes first.

For more information on the Friends of PM, and about sponsoring particular projects, please go to www.pmpress.org, or contact us at info@pmpress.org.